The Secret Astoria Scavenger Hunt

By Susan Colleen Browne

Morgan Carey and The Curse of the Corpse Bride

The Mystery of the Christmas Fairies
A Morgan Carey Adventure

The Secret Astoria Scavenger Hunt
A Morgan Carey Adventure

The Secret Astoria Scavenger Hunt

A Morgan Carey Adventure, Book 3

SUSAN COLLEEN BROWNE

The Secret Astoria Scavenger Hunt

eBook ISBN: 978-0-9967408-1-4
Print ISBN: 978-0-9967408-2-1

www.susancolleenbrowne.com
www.littlefarminthefoothills.blogspot.com

Cover design by E-book Formatting Fairies
Interior formatting by Author E.M.S.

Library of Congress Control Number: 2015914925

Published in the United States of America.

For

The Three Astoria Musketeers,

Meghan, Seamus and Rowan

1

The Skeleton in the Floor

The human skeleton dangled from an invisible cord beneath a clear floor panel, light from the nearby fireplace flickering on the top of its skull. Shivering, Morgan tore her eyes from the creepy hole at her feet. "Guys! Come see this!" She stepped around a sign on a metal stand that said, *Proud Sponsor of "The Goonies" Anniversary Celebration,* and waved at her cousins, sitting at a table at the Smuggler's Hole Café.

"I'm drawing," said Sean without looking up.

Ronan slid from his chair, scooting over to join Morgan. "What's going on?"

"Look at that!"

Ronan peered into the dim pit, covered with a hard plastic square. "You don't think the skeleton is *real*, do you?"

"It's fake, of course." Morgan tried to sound casual, though her heart beat faster. After that strange Halloween she'd had back in the fifth grade, she knew that even unbelievable things can happen to you—and it can be awfully hard to figure out what's true and what's made up. "I mean, what kind of restaurant would have a human skeleton in a hole, except as a joke?"

Ronan stepped onto the plastic panel and jumped on it. "Ronan!" hissed Morgan. Almost ten, Ronan could be a little *too* mischievous. "You'll break it! And get us into trouble—"

"No, look, it's solid," said Ronan. "Like, double super-glued." He called to his big brother, "Sean—come over here!"

"Got to finish this first," Sean said. Morgan hid a smile. Sean, just turned eleven, was the kind of kid who got completely absorbed in whatever he was doing. And when he was *really* into something, the whole world could blow up and he would hardly notice.

"We watched *The Goonies* again last night, to get ready for this weekend," said Ronan. "I guess Sean got all inspired to draw a picture about the movie."

"I watched it too, before we left home," Morgan told him. She and her mom were visiting her aunt's family in the small riverside town of Astoria, Oregon, for *The Goonies* Anniversary Celebration. "I can't wait to go to all the events tomorrow! You're so lucky to live here."

"You mean 'cause *The Goonies* was filmed in Astoria?" asked Ronan. "Yeah, it's pretty cool. Every time Sean and I watch the movie we look for the real places around town."

He eyed the panel like he wanted to stomp on it again.

"Don't even *think* about it," Morgan warned. "The last thing we need is to get grounded, when we've got all kinds of Anniversary plans." Now that she was almost thirteen, starting eighth grade in the fall, naturally her mom was bringing her along to all the parties.

"All *right*," said Ronan, pretending to pout.

"My dad teases me and Mom that the movie is just a dorky fantasy, but we think the whole weekend is going to be a blast!" Morgan peeked at the skeleton one last time. It seemed to move a tiny bit, like it was being shaken by an invisible hand. "Uh, Ronan, there's something..."

He'd already turned toward the table. "Sean!" he called again. "Will you just get over—"

"Never mind." Morgan shook her head as if to clear it. Seeing this skeleton *and* knowing she had two whole days in the world of *The Goonies* had her imagination working overtime. "We'll get him to look at the hole on our way out."

They ambled back to the table, the worn floorboards creaking under Morgan's feet. The Café was located in one of the oldest structures in town, built on a wooden pier that extended directly over the Columbia River. A summer evening breeze drifted through the Café's open windows, smelling briny and sea-weedy, and Morgan could hear the river lapping against the wood pilings. Her gaze wandered back to the area around the hole. Her aunt said that part was built right over the river. *I'll bet if I went over there and stomped on the plastic, harder than Ronan, the floor would open up and I'd fall right next to that skeleton.* She shivered again.

Now that the restaurant was nearly deserted, the grownups didn't mind if Morgan and her cousins roamed around. Besides, Morgan's mom Nicole, and her sister, Morgan's Aunt Shannon—Sean and Ronan's mom—were acting kind of like kids too. They were chattering non-stop about all *The Goonies* events around town.

"What are you wearing to the Eighties party?" Aunt Shannon asked Morgan's mom. She was cuddling Mary Rose, the boys' baby sister.

Her mom's eyes sparkled. "A blue Superman t-shirt, red suspenders and cut-offs—what else?"

"*The Goonies'* 'Sloth' character!" said Aunt Shannon. "It's so you."

"Oh, *Mom.*" Morgan laughed. "I think you'd time travel back to 1985 if you could."

"Absolutely." Her mom giggled, reaching over to tickle Mary Rose's cheek. "Do you think your mommy and I would miss a chance to relive *The Goonies'* experience?" she asked the baby.

The whole town was already going crazy. On the way to the Café, Morgan had seen a ton of people—mostly grownups—in costumes from the movie. "What's really great," Morgan told Mary Rose, "is that *The Goonies* will be playing at the town's theatre all weekend, so we can see it as many times as we want!"

Mary Rose wiggled like she was excited about watching the movie. She stuck her thumb in her mouth and looked at her brothers.

Sean was sketching a bunch of lines on his paper, while Ronan pulled a small book from his jeans pocket. Morgan tilted her head to read the title. *A Mini-Guidebook: Facts and Legends about Astoria, Oregon.* She took out her phone and keyed in the site of *The Goonies* Anniversary Celebration. What was completely awesome was that a few celebrities—cast and crew from the movie—were going to be at the events too.

"I thought we'd have to cancel our visit this weekend," Mom was saying. "Every hotel and motel was booked solid! I finally found a B&B downtown that had some space."

"What's the name of it?" Aunt Shannon asked. Mary Rose sucked her thumb vigorously.

"It's a beautiful Victorian house," Mom said, grinning. "It's got lots of gingerbread trim, and a cute little garden shed in the backyard."

"The shed's built against a small hill," said Morgan, "kind of like a Hobbit's house!"

"Really, it's just darling," said her mom. "Apparently the original owner's great-great-granddaughter recently bought the house!"

"Which B&B?" Aunt Shannon persisted.

"Hang on." Morgan held up one hand, then pulled up the B&B website. "Here it is." She leaned over to show her aunt.

THE LAHTI HOUSE BED & BREAKFAST
Charming and cozy accommodations with a River View,
in the Heart of Historical Astoria!
Vintage Board games available to guests.
Afternoon high tea upon request.

Aunt Shannon seemed to go tense. "I thought so. The Lahti House."

Mary Rose stopped sucking her thumb.

"It's great, isn't it?" Morgan closed the site, and brought up the website for the town of Astoria.

"They even have extra rooms available." Morgan's mom finished her iced tea. "You and your hubby and the baby could get a room there and another for the boys—we could be together all weekend!"

"Um," said Aunt Shannon. She looked away.

Mom set down her glass. "What? Is something the matter with it?" She made a face. "Crummy breakfasts? They advertised French toast and fresh fruit—"

Aunt Shannon shook her head. "Didn't you wonder why no one else is staying at the B&B?"

"The beds are lumpy?" Aunt Shannon didn't say anything. Mom went on, "Not...Morgan, don't get grossed out—not bedbugs?"

"You wish," said Aunt Shannon. She peeped at the boys, who were still preoccupied, and put her hand on the side of her face. "People say," and she dropped her voice to a whisper, "that The Lahti House is...haunted."

2

The Contest

"Haunted? Oh, come on," said Morgan's mom. She wasn't worried about Morgan listening in and getting creeped out. Morgan loved scary movies, scary books, and telling bloodcurdling stories at slumber parties. She knew all the party stories were only urban legends or whatever, but they were more fun than movie-watching!

Her mom shook her head. "A haunted bed-and-breakfast—it's such a cliché! Besides, you don't actually believe all those Astoria tall tales?"

"They're *not* tall tales," said Aunt Shannon. She was big on mystical things like fairies, Ouija boards, and all those ghost-hunting TV shows. "I've heard that back in the day, there were some mysterious disappearances from the house." She kissed Mary Rose's fuzzy head. "People have just up and...vanished."

"It sounds ridiculous," Mom said. "The stories are just a ploy—publicity to get more tourists here." She tugged playfully on a strand of Morgan's long brown hair. "You don't believe them either, do you, Sweetie?"

"Um...no," said Morgan. *Although after I had that weird Halloween curse put on me, I know the freakiest things can be...well, real.* Not that she'd ever tell her mom what had happened two years ago. She wasn't going to mention either, that when she and her mom brought their suitcases into their B&B room a little while ago, she'd had the strangest feeling. As if she was being...watched. "There's one thing about The Lahti House, though."

"What?" asked Aunt Shannon. Mary Rose began making fussy sounds.

"Mom, didn't you notice it?" Morgan asked.

"Notice what?"

"The B&B looks huge from the outside," Morgan said. "But when we went up to our room, I could tell that inside, the house isn't very big."

"My point *exactly*," said Aunt Shannon. She shifted the baby to her shoulder. "The house is just strange."

"What does smuggling mean?" Ronan asked suddenly. "My book says there was lots of it going on in Astoria, in the olden days."

Morgan's mom glanced at his book. "Smuggling is when people sneak stuff in or out of a place that they're not supposed to."

"What kind of stuff?" asked Ronan.

"Well," Mom said, "It's generally things some people

might want, even though those things might be bad for them. Or for the environment. Like...oh, drugs. Or ivory from elephant tusks."

"I understand there was a lot of fur smuggling going on in Astoria's early history," said Aunt Shannon, rubbing the baby's back.

"Smugglers might use trucks or planes or boats to move their goods, then sell them for big money," said Mom. "But they do it secretly."

"You mean smuggling is against the law?" Ronan's eyes gleamed.

"That's right," confirmed her mom.

"In Astoria, the smugglers used ships," said Ronan. "Listen to this. 'They were dangerous, ruthless desperados, stopping at nothing to ferry their booty to those willing to pay outrageous prices for it.'"

"What kind of booty?" asked Sean.

Ronan scanned the page. "I haven't gotten to that part."

"Gold and silver and jewels, I bet," said Sean. "Like in *The Goonies.*"

Mary Rose lifted her head to look at her brother.

"It makes you wonder if the people who dreamed up the movie were inspired by real history," Aunt Shannon remarked. "Astoria does have quite the colorful past."

"Like with Lewis and Clark," Sean put in.

"What I love about living here is being around all the historical buildings," Aunt Shannon went on. "I understand the one we're in—the Café here—is over a hundred years old. It used to be the Riverside Mercantile."

"What's a mercantile, Mom?" Ronan asked.

"A general store," Aunt Shannon told him. The baby nestled her downy head against her mommy's neck. "And did you know the Astoria arcade is really old too? It was once a men's clothing store."

"Neat," said Ronan, and went back to his book.

"Every day, I get to drive past the old county jail and the Victorian homes," Morgan's aunt said. "It's living history."

"Speaking of old houses," said Morgan, waving her phone, "The Lahti House isn't the only place that's weird. Some of the articles I've been looking at on the town's website are a little suspicious."

"Oh, come on," said her mom. "Your auntie hasn't been talking you into believing all those crazy Astoria stories?"

"Um..." Morgan put her phone into her pocket. Her mom was *so* not into supernatural or paranormal stuff. And since she refused to believe strange things really could happen, Morgan didn't want to be the one to burst her bubble. "What do you think, Auntie?"

"The stories aren't crazy," said Aunt Shannon, patting Mary Rose's diapered bottom. The baby went back to sucking her thumb.

"Shannon..." began Mom.

"All I'm saying, is there are plenty of things that have happened in Astoria that no one's been able to explain," said

Aunt Shannon. "You know what they say, where there's smoke, there's fire."

Morgan's mom rolled her eyes. "You *know* that people in this town play up all that—"

"I may have a wild imagination," said Aunt Shannon with a dignified look, "but it's not that wild. And like I said, The Lahti House does have a reputation."

Frowning, Mom gathered up her purse. "It's way past the kids' bedtime."

Morgan still felt wide awake. And the boys didn't seem sleepy either. "Did you know that in the olden days, Astoria had *two* big fires?" said Ronan. He leaned toward his brother, showing him a page.

Sean set the book next to his paper and jotted down a couple more things. He finally looked up, blinking like he was coming out of a long nap. "I've been drawing a map for you, Aunt Nicky," he said.

"A map of what?" said Morgan's mom.

"Of Astoria," said Sean. "While you're visiting, Auntie, you'll be able to find all the good places to go."

Morgan and her mom studied Sean's map. "Astoria" was scrawled in big looping letters at the top of the page, and beneath it was a cluster of houses and two wide, curving parallel lines. Between the lines he'd written, "Columbia River," with train tracks and a little trolley alongside the river. Three long piers jutted into where the water was supposed to be, and next to one dock there was a collection of round creatures. They had to be Astoria's famous sea lions you could hear *ark, arking* all over town, day or night.

Aunt Shannon leaned over for a look. "I see you've got some of the town's most famous buildings on your map too, honey."

"Yeah," said Sean. Next to each one, he'd drawn an arrow pointing to the name of the place, like the old Freedom movie theatre, the Astoria Column, the Oregon Film Museum, the Smuggler's Hole Café, and his and Ronan's favorite spots: the Columbia River Maritime Museum and the arcade downtown. He'd even sketched in the Lahti B&B.

Morgan's mom broke into a smile. "Sean—this is amazing!" She put her arm around him and gave him a hug. "We won't get lost with a map like this."

"Wow, it's great," said Morgan, impressed. Seeing Sean's B&B picture, though, she wondered if he had been listening to the talk about the supposedly haunted house. "Come see what Ronan and I wanted to show you—you might want to add it to the map."

Sean stuck his pencil into his jeans pocket and neatly rolled up the map. Handing the paper to Morgan, he said, "Take good care of it," and followed her and Ronan toward the fireplace. She stuck the map roll into her hoodie pocket, and pointed to the dark, square cavity. "A fake skeleton," she said, before he could get any ideas. Although Sean was a year older than Ronan, he got weirded out a little more easily.

He surprised her by crouching next to the Plexiglas panel, and peering intently into the hole. Morgan said in a rush, "I was telling Ronan that the skeleton's plastic—it's just a gag, to fill the dark box—"

"Say, kids." One of the café's servers came over, a smiling woman with pink streaks in her hair. She held a small leather case in one hand and a sheet of paper in the other. "I wanted to tell you about something special."

"We just ate, thanks," Morgan said politely.

"It's not a food special, it's a special event," said the pink-haired lady. "To celebrate *The Goonies* Anniversary, the Café is running a contest about that skeleton!"

"Cool," said Ronan.

"What's the contest?" asked Sean, rising to his feet. "Is it about geometry? I'm sort of good at that."

"Actually, the contest is called 'Name the Skeleton.' We want to see who can come up with the best name for the skeleton down there, along with a story about how it got there!" said the server. "I brought you an entry form in case you're interested."

"Are you kidding me?" said Sean, his face lighting up. "I want to enter."

"Me too," chimed in Ronan. "My brother and I can do it together."

"The contest is for kids twelve and under." Ms. Pink

Hair handed Sean the paper. "Now I'll just get your moms' bill," she said and hurried to their table. Morgan could hear her saying, "There are so many adults who go nuts about *The Goonies* celebration, so we wanted to do something fun just for kids."

Sean bent his head over the entry form, Morgan and Ronan crowding in to read it too.

"So," said Ronan, "it says you have to write a story about the skeleton—who it was, and how it got into the hole, and the most creative story wins. Sounds easy!"

"But look," said Morgan. "The contest is on just for *The Goonies* weekend. You've only got until tomorrow night to enter."

"Let's go for it," Sean said. "Look at this—if you win, you get your picture in the newspaper and they print your story too!"

"Wait—there's more!" Ronan hopped around with excitement. "The winner gets a certificate at the closing ceremonies of *The Goonies* Anniversary!" He folded up the entry form to stick in the pocket of his sweatshirt. "Sean—if we win, we'll be famous! Morgan, you'll help us, won't you?"

Morgan grinned at her cousins. If they wanted to be Astoria celebs, who was she to stand in their way? "Sure—I'm not thirteen until next month. But I want you guys to win the contest with your own ideas. Do you have any yet?"

"The skeleton could have been a pirate," said Ronan. "But I'll bet everyone will use that. I mean, *The Goonies* movie was about pirates, especially that guy with one eye."

"Yeah, we can think of something better." Sean glanced back at the floor panel, looking thoughtful. "I just got an idea..."

"What?" asked Ronan. "Something for the contest?"

"I dunno," said Sean, "but I was thinking there could be a mystery about this hole."

"Isn't it just part of the crawlspace?" asked Morgan. Then she remembered something. If the restaurant was built on top of the river, when the tide came in, wouldn't there be... *water* beneath the skeleton?

"What if whatever is down there is more than just a hole?" asked Sean. "Ronan's book mentioned there are some legends in Astoria about underground passages."

"Passages?" Morgan echoed.

"You know. Tunnels."

Ronan's eyes widened. "To where?"

"That's what I'd like to figure out." Sean stared into the hole again, then pulled out his pencil. "Can I see my map?"

Mystified, Morgan handed it over. Sean unrolled the map, and crouching, set it on the Plexiglas. He studied his paper for a few seconds, then began to draw. A moment later, he sat back on his heels, showing the map to Morgan and Ronan. "Here's my theory—I think somebody—"

"A desperado," put in Ronan. "Some kind of crook."

"Yeah," agreed Sean. "They could have come through a tunnel from one of these places. See?"

He'd added more skinny parallel lines. One set led from the Smuggler's Hole Café to the Freedom Theatre. Another two sets of lines ran from the middle of Astoria, one to the theatre and another back to the Café. Finally, he'd scratched an arrow with the word "tunnel" next to each.

"Oh," said Morgan slowly. The tunnels formed a perfect triangle.

3

All Shook Up

"*D*id you feel the quake last night?" asked Valerie, the cheerful older woman who owned the B&B.

"Earthquake?" Sitting in the bright kitchen of The Lahti House, Morgan dropped the B&B brochure she was reading. Maybe there had been a small tremblor while she'd been at the Café—so she really *had* seen the skeleton move!

"Right here in Astoria?" Morgan's mom clutched her cloth napkin.

"I'm afraid so. My neighbor is a police officer, and she stopped by early this morning to tell me it hit around midnight." Valerie set a bowl of fresh strawberries on the round antique table, the sweet, fruity smell filling the room. "The area hasn't had any earthquakes for years, so to have one happen now, when there are thousands of visitors in town—well!"

"Was anyone hurt?" asked Mom, looking alarmed.

"No, thank goodness. Apparently the damage was

minimal too," said Valerie. "Except—can you believe this? At the Smuggler's Hole Café—you know, the place with the skeleton in the floor—the quake blew the plastic panel right off the hole!"

"That's pretty weird," said Morgan. The panel had sure seemed secure when Ronan had jumped on it.

"Anyway," Valerie went on, "even if everyone in town got a little shaken, the Anniversary Celebration is going just as planned."

Morgan, spooning fresh strawberries on her French toast, exchanged a relieved glance with her mom. "You didn't get any breakage here at the B&B?" asked Mom.

"It's kind of amazing," said Valerie. "This house is full of antiques and heirloom knickknacks, but everything looks okay. I was really lucky—an old house like this isn't earthquake-proof."

With the morning sunlight streaming through the wavy glass of the kitchen door, just like any other day, Morgan decided the quake couldn't have been that big a deal. As she and her mom started eating their breakfasts, she picked up the B&B brochure again.

...The Lahti Bed-and-Breakfast is named for the architect of the home, Mr. Robert Lahti. Astoria's most famous builder from the early twentieth century, Mr. Lahti also designed the Freedom Theatre, the Men's Haberdashery building, now the Astoria arcade, and the

Riverside Mercantile, currently the Smuggler's Hole Café...

Morgan opened the brochure, and stared at a photo inside. She took another brochure from the stack, opened it, then a third, and opened it too. *Uh oh.*

"Morgan, one brochure is enough," her mom said, taking a bite of French toast.

"Oh, feel free to take a few with you," said Valerie, pouring a cup of dried beans into a slow cooker. "I just got them from the printers this week—I'd love to get the word out about my new B&B."

"I hate to tell you," said Morgan, "but someone's been, um, messing around with them." She showed the three brochures to Valerie, pointing to the photo with the caption, *Mr. Lahti's family at the celebration of his eldest daughter's fourteenth birthday.* Someone's head had been cut out of the photo.

"Oh no!" said Valerie, staring hard at the photo. She grabbed the stack of brochures from their holder on the table and opened a handful. Morgan could see that each brochure had the same head cut out. Valerie's face crumbled. "They're all ruined!"

Mom looked over. "Who would do that? Cut someone's face out of the photo?"

Valerie set the brochures down, turning toward the sink. "My daughter brought my little grandson over a couple of days ago. He must've gotten a hold of some scissors—he's three, you know, in that destructive phase. He always makes a terrible mess in my kitchen."

Morgan bit her lip. The faces had been cut in a near perfect circle. "I don't think a three-year-old could—"

"Morgan." Her mom looked at her with a tiny shake of her head. "I used to do naughty things like that when I was little," she said to Valerie. "Don't worry, we'll be happy to tell people about your B&B."

"Would you?" Valerie said gratefully. She filled a large metal measuring cup with water and poured it into the crock. "I've been thinking maybe people prefer going to modern motels, because I've..." A worried look crossed her face. "I've had a hard time getting guests here."

Morgan felt a jolt of excitement. "Is it because your house is haun—"

"We'd better finish breakfast," her mom said quickly. "I don't want to be late for the tour of *The Goonies* locations—it starts in an hour."

Valerie seemed to force a smile. "They're saying this year's Celebration is going to be the best yet!"

"My sister and I are *huge* fans of the movie," said Mom, taking her last bite of French toast. "We've signed up for every event."

"So you won't be needing tea this afternoon?" asked Valerie, plugging in the slow cooker. "I'll be able to go to a few events myself then." The woman didn't look all that excited, though. "I'll lock the front and back doors, but your room key will open both." She seemed to hesitate. "Sorry to dump my problems on you, but I have to admit I may not be able to keep the B&B going much longer."

"Try not to get discouraged," said Mom. "Every new business needs time to get rolling."

"I'm sure you're right," said Valerie, although she looked anything but sure. "Do you need anything else before you go?"

"We're good." Mom rose from the table and gave Valerie's arm a comforting pat. "Maybe my sister and I will run into you at some Anniversary event." She avoided Morgan's eyes as they returned upstairs.

Suddenly, the *unthinkable* dawned on Morgan—she wasn't invited.

4

Not Grown Up

"I can't believe you're not taking me to *The Goonies* Celebration!" Morgan dashed angry tears from her eyes before her mom could see.

Slouched in front of the window seat in their room, Morgan shoved her hands in her jeans pockets and looked out at the river, just blocks away. Fog rose from the water, drifting around the Megler Bridge leading to Washington State. For a moment, the tall bridge seemed to disappear, then seconds later, it reappeared through the mist. "You always say I'm more mature than most high school kids!"

"Sweetie, don't be like that." Her mom sat before the old-fashioned vanity table in her Sloth costume, winding her curling iron around a strand of hair. Humming Cindy Lauper's "Girls Just Wanna Have Fun," she leaned closer to the mirror. "I'll take you to a bunch of events tomorrow."

But I want to go today! Morgan turned from the window and stared around the room. It was pretty, if you liked girly-frilly décor—a lace-edged quilt on the queen-sized bed, lace curtains, and a flowered china bowl and pitcher on one side of the vanity. She didn't mind girliness in small doses, but right now the frills and lace bugged her like crazy.

Actually, *everything* was bugging her. For something to do, Morgan stomped to the nightstand and jerked open a drawer. Inside was a silver-backed hairbrush, some blond hairs stuck in the bristles. *No wonder Valerie doesn't have more customers, if she leaves someone's old hairbrush around!* She slammed the drawer shut, feeling like a little kid ready to throw a tantrum.

Her problem was, she'd never exactly asked her mom if she could go to the celebration—she'd just assumed it.

Her mom took her to a lot of places Morgan's friends didn't get to go to—concerts, theatre shows, and once in a while, a girls' night dinner with her mom and grownup friends. She did feel a lot older than her girlfriends from school. Unlike the girls she hung out with, Morgan had big plans for the future. She couldn't *wait* to learn to drive, and get a job. And not just babysit, like her friends. Morgan had grander ideas: she was going to start her own business. She was totally ready to grow up!

She absently pushed on the bridge of her nose, then remembered she didn't have glasses anymore. "Didn't you decide I was old enough to get contacts? So why can't I go today?"

"Do I need to explain the whole thing again?" her mom asked patiently.

"Okay, we drove all the way from Seattle so I could sit around Aunt Shannon's house with the boys, doing nothing!" Morgan scowled. "Zilch!" She'd known that Uncle Jake, her aunt's husband, was taking care of Mary Rose and the boys, so Aunt Shannon would be free for the afternoon. Little did Morgan know Uncle Jake would be *babysitting* her too! She added, "Do nothing *and* be completely bored!"

Mom curled the last lock of her hair, still smiling. "Honey, can you just chill?"

Morgan could tell her mom was too excited to seriously scold her. "And it's so unbelievable that you're not taking me to *The Goonies'* treasure hunt!" Gathering her hair into one hand, Morgan chose a purple elastic band from the ones she'd left on the vanity. She made a ponytail, snapping the band into place. "It's going to be so awesome! What am I, a baby—like Mary Rose? Or Valerie's grandson who's not even old enough to handle scissors?"

"Of course you're not," said her mom, putting away her curling iron. "But your auntie's been at home an awful lot since Mary Rose was born, with hardly a break for months. She needs some kid-free time."

I'm not a kid! Morgan wanted to say. Only there was no getting around that she still had another month to go, before she would be a real teenager. "If you take me today it can be my early birthday present," she coaxed. "I won't even ask for a birthday party."

Her mom looked thoughtful. "How about this—if you feel ready for more independence, you can take the boys to the arcade. Then the three of you can walk back here and spend the afternoon on your own."

The thought of being stuck at the B&B all afternoon while her mom had all the fun still made her want to scream or something. But she and the boys could probably come up with more interesting things to do here than sitting at Aunt Shannon's house.

"I guess," Morgan said grudgingly as her mom pulled out her phone. She yanked a clean hoodie over her head and slid her arms through it. Pulling Sean's map out of the top she'd worn last night, she stuck it in her pocket. *At least Mom thinks I'm old enough to hang out with my cousins in the hotel room—without an adult.*

Walking the three blocks to the arcade with her mom, Morgan stepped carefully on the crowded sidewalks to avoid crashing into anyone. Downtown Astoria was jammed with people, and like yesterday, many of them wore costumes. She decided pirates were the most popular—a couple of guys' outfits were so authentic they were wearing those high, fold-over boots like Johnny Depp's in *Pirates of the Caribbean*. Marine Drive was a complete snarl, and she could hear *The Goonies* soundtrack music blaring from some car windows.

When Morgan and her mom arrived at the arcade, Aunt Shannon and the boys were already standing out front. She leaned in to give Morgan a hug, and whispered, "I see no ghosts got you last night."

Smiling in anticipation, Aunt Shannon was all dressed up in a glittery top and pencil skirt, with a big eighties hairdo. Morgan had to admit that her aunt probably did need an afternoon away. But she was too bummed about missing today's treasure hunt to enjoy her aunt's joke. "Heh, heh," she said.

"You guys heard about the quake?" asked Aunt Shannon. She seemed more excited than nervous. "I checked my Facebook feed this morning, and found out that a little over a hundred years ago, one of the biggest earthquakes in Astoria's history hit the town! That one did some serious damage, and there were even some aftershocks."

"Fires, smugglers, now earthquakes," Mom remarked. "Astoria is turning out to be kind of a dangerous place."

"Yeah, maybe someone should wind yellow 'Caution' tape around the town," said Ronan.

"Now there's an idea," Morgan's mom said, smiling at him. "I guess we're lucky this earthquake wasn't a lot worse."

"For us, not the Smuggler's Hole Café," said Aunt Shannon.

"You're talking about that floor panel over the skeleton? We heard it blew off," said Morgan's mom. "It freaks me out that we were only a few feet away from it last night!"

"There's more," said Sean. "Mom heard the skeleton got stolen after the floor exploded!"

"Nothing really exploded, honey," Aunt Shannon began. "But did you know, there's a full moon?"

"Oh, you and your full moon ideas," said Mom. Aunt Shannon was really big on unexplainable things happening when the moon was full. "Next you'll be telling us you saw a werewolf."

"You can laugh," said Aunt Shannon, lifting a well-shaped eyebrow at her sister, "but it's not only the full moon, but a *blue* moon. Double the power of the—"

"I saw the moon this morning," said Sean. "And it wasn't blue. Not even close."

"Sean, the blue moon isn't actually the color blue," Aunt Shannon told him. "It's called a blue moon when there are two full moons during a calendar month. Anyway, no wonder a bunch of strange things went on."

"Do you think the skeleton contest will still be on?" asked Ronan, looking anxious.

Morgan saw her mom and aunt exchange a glance—she noticed grownups often looked at each other when they didn't want to tell kids what was really going on. Aunt Shannon stepped a little distance away.

"I'm sure it is, Sweetie," said Morgan's mom. "I'll bet the

missing skeleton was just a prank—with the Anniversary Celebration going on, there are some really...um, interesting characters visiting Astoria." She cut her eyes toward another passersby, who had a black eyepatch drawn on his face with a marker. "Whoever stole the skeleton will probably return it over the weekend. In the meantime, are you all ready for the arcade?"

"Sean and I each got ten dollars," Ronan told her. "We can play forty games!"

"Some games take two tokens," Sean said. "So if you play those games, you only get twenty of—"

"Either way, I'm sure you'll have loads of fun," said Morgan's mom.

"Oh, yay," said Morgan, feeling grumpy all over again. "Not as much fun as we'd have at *The Goonies'* celebration," she added under her breath.

Aunt Shannon rejoined them. "I just called the Café, and the contest is definitely still on. They're super bummed, though. The skeleton was the whole focus of their promotion. Anyhoo—Nicky, let's go!"

"Your phone is charged up?" her mom asked as Aunt Shannon kissed the boys goodbye.

"Yeah," said Morgan, putting on her sulkiest face while her mom was still around. There was no point of sulking if your parents were gone.

"And you'll be careful, right?"

"As if anything could happen to us in a place full of

people." Morgan pulled out her phone to double-check the charge. "Or stuck in some old B&B."

"Great!" said her mom, then she frowned slightly. "By the way, keep track of that B&B key."

Morgan yanked the key from her jeans pocket, showing it to her mom. "I'm old enough not to lose a key!"

As she shoved it back in, her mom said to Aunt Shannon, "Can you believe they only gave us one?"

Aunt Shannon gave her sister the eyebrow look again. "I told you the place was...odd."

"It's weird, all right," said Morgan. "I've got to tell you about their brochu—"

"You can tell your aunt later." Mom gave her a kiss. "Call us if you need anything," she said gaily, and she and Aunt Shannon walked away without a backward look.

Morgan watched the two of them make a beeline for the old jail, now the Oregon Film Museum, and realized she'd forgotten to give Sean's map to them. She patted her hoodie pocket, where it was still rolled up. *Well, if Mom gets separated from Aunt Shannon and can't find her way around, too bad!* Morgan thought. *She should have taken me along!*

5

Cinderella's Stepsister

"Nothing exciting ever happens to me," Morgan complained two hours later.

Lounging around the B&B room with Sean and Ronan, she was still in a crummy mood, despite their successful morning at the arcade. She and her cousins had won dozens of tickets, redeeming them for a few of those super-cheapo toys and gizmos arcades specialized in. Morgan found most of the prizes were sort of silly—she'd ended up choosing two of the least dorky items in the display.

One was a decorative candle in the shape of a sea lion, about three inches high. She figured she could give it to Aunt Shannon. The other was an old fashioned key that looked almost exactly like the one from their B&B room, the kind people called...whatchacallit? Skeleton keys.

Morgan didn't have any use for the key, but her best friend Claire might like it. Claire's favorite piece of jewelry was a charm bracelet that had lots of clunky doodads attached with wire—the junkier the better—and she could use the key for another charm. She wanted to be a professional singer when she grew up—an *artist*.

"If you're unusual you have more of a chance of being famous," Claire had said more than once. "Besides, my bracelet makes sort of a statement, until the day my mom lets me wear lots of lipstick and black eyeliner."

Anyway, when Morgan and her cousins returned to the B&B earlier, she ended up not needing the room key at all. A snarky girl showed up at the front door to let them inside. Which was odd, since Valerie hadn't mentioned any extra helpers at her B&B—she'd implied she couldn't afford to hire staff. So the girl had to be another problem grandchild, because she acted like she owned the place. In fact, she was so bossy and superior that Morgan, who liked to think she was pretty easygoing, had wanted to pop her one!

Now, Morgan pushed the girl from her mind, sighing as Ronan rolled the dice in their third game of Clue. Or was it their fourth? She was so bored she'd lost track. If Morgan had been in a better mood she would've thought this old version of the game was pretty cool. Although the board illustrations were faded, the designs were more layered and shadowy, and the weapons were made of metal and plastic. Sean had turned down Clue to shoot baskets with his arcade prize, a green glow-in-the-dark Nerf ball and a suction-cup basket he'd stuck to the wall. And Ronan might as well be playing Clue alone, because Morgan couldn't get into the game at all.

"Nothing exciting ever happens to you?" Ronan picked a Clue card, a crafty expression on his freckled face. Near the board was the mini-flashlight he'd won at the arcade.

"No," said Morgan. "Never." She shifted on the bed. "Actually..." her voice trailed away.

She couldn't tell her cousin about the eerie Halloween experience she'd had a couple of years ago. She wasn't going to mention either, the holiday visit to her grandparents' house that same year. She'd been there all day Christmas Eve, yet her mind was a total blank about how she'd passed the time. But she had the strangest feeling— actually just the faintest sensation—that she'd gone into the woods and sort of disappeared into a mist. Then all of a sudden she was back in her grandma's garden. She hadn't even told Claire about that. Not that she had much to say about it, since she had no memory...

"Exciting stuff happens to *me*," said Ronan, and he triumphantly moved his game piece across the board. "Like winning! Miss Scarlett did it in the bedroom with the pistol!" He picked up the tiny metal pistol, pointed it at the window and made an explosive sound. "Pquoo!"

Morgan examined her cards and game sheet. "Aw, Ronan, you win again!" she said, faking her disappointment. It had been Ronan's idea to play Clue, to inspire them for the Café contest, but she was really sick of playing. Maybe she could talk Ronan into something that was actually...fun. "What should we do now?" She lay back on the bed, and the sea lion candle in her back pocket made an uncomfortable lump. She rolled aside to move the candle to her hoodie pocket.

"Tell ghost stories?" Ronan grabbed the flashlight. Clicking it on, he set it against his chin, shining it upward. "Do I look scary?" Then he shone it in Morgan's eyes.

"Aw, cut it out," said Morgan, sitting back up. "It's more fun if you tell the stories when it's dark."

As Ronan clicked the flashlight off, Sean said, "How about a basketball tournament? After we get the room cooled down, that is." He climbed on the window seat to open the window, then jumped off toward the vanity table. Grabbing the chair in front of the table, he scraped it across the floor to the wall where he'd stuck the basket.

"Shhhh!" said Morgan. "You don't want that awful girl to come up and bug us!"

"Actually," said Sean, clambering up on the chair to move the basket as high as he could reach. "I didn't think she was awful. Just...mysterious."

For all her snarkiness, the kid who'd let them into the B&B earlier had been the prettiest girl Morgan had ever seen. She was about the same age as Morgan, maybe a year older but much smaller, with long blond curly hair, clear, light skin and big blue eyes. She was dressed in a lacy white dress that looked like some kind of costume, similar to what the women wore in the B&B brochure photo.

Despite the odd clothing, the girl was beautiful enough to be one of the real-life "princesses" you could take your picture with at Disneyland. Except—the rest of her was a mess. Her hair was matted, she had a smudge of dirt on one cheek, and the dress was creased and faded, as if it had been worn for *years* without being washed. She looked like Cinderella before the Fairy Godmother had done her magic.

"Hey," Morgan had said to the girl.

"You live here too?" asked Ronan. Sean just stared at her, speechless. Morgan grinned to herself. Her cousin was just getting to the age where he was noticing girls.

Instead of smiling a greeting, the girl stood in the middle of the doorway, blocking their passage. "Which room?" she said sharply. For a girl, she had *really* husky voice.

"Um, Room Seven?" said Morgan, taken aback. "The Tower Room?"

"On the top floor," Ronan put in.

The girl scowled. "Not Room Seven! No one stays in Room Seven."

"I think I know which room we're in," Morgan retorted. Her mom had taught her not to let rude people intimidate her. At least not too much.

"Why are you asking my cousin what room she's in?" said

Sean, finding his voice. "You have to know she and her mom are the only people staying here." He liked to keep the facts straight.

"Show me the key," said the girl. Her voice was even more gravelly than the old woman villain in *The Goonies* movie.

"You look kind of like a fairy tale princess," observed Sean.

The girl ignored him. "The key!"

Morgan sighed, and reached into her right jeans pocket. Quickly changing her mind, she stifled another grin and pulled her arcade key from her other pocket. "See? Room Seven."

The girl squinted at the key. "Hmmm. I really must give you a different room," she said in her raspy voice. "Room Three should do."

"No it won't," said Morgan. This girl was like, so inappropriate! "You have to ask my mom first."

The girl stared at her with narrowed eyes. "Perhaps I'll let you keep Room Seven," she said, her lip curling. She handed back the key and finally moved aside. "For now," she added in a foreboding tone.

"Thanks," Morgan said sarcastically.

"But only if you're very quiet," the girl said, her gaze shifting from Morgan to the boys, looking so intense her eyes seemed to burn. "I'm quite busy and need to concentrate."

"*Whatev*," said Morgan, brushing past the girl. She and the boys barely made it upstairs and inside the room before they burst into laughter. "Is she for real?" Morgan asked, giggling. Most hotel employees were the smiley-est people ever. "I thought she was like Cinderella, but she could actually be one of the wicked stepsisters."

"Esmerelda!" Sean chuckled. "Except she's not ugly!"

"And did you notice?" Morgan giggled harder. "She talks like she's pretending to be on..." She thought of her aunt's favorite show. "*Downton Abbey* or something."

"She looks like she swallowed a whole bag of sour patch candy," said Ronan, grinning, which made them burst into more giggles.

Sean was the first to stop laughing. "Wait—maybe she's in the *Shanghaied in Astoria* play this year. And she didn't get a chance to change to her regular clothes."

The play was one of the town's biggest events—a locally produced musical comedy that was performed every summer. The boys had probably attended the show six times. The theatre sold popcorn for super-cheap, and part of the fun was that audience members were encouraged to throw popcorn at the actors, the more the better. Morgan had thrown at least a couple of buckets of it onstage the last time she'd attended.

"You're probably right," said Morgan. "I bet rehearsals are going on now."

Claire had acted in some musical plays at school. She

said real actors—she'd called them *artists* too—stay in character like, 24/7, until the film or play is over. One time Claire had played a character for a whole weekend, driving Morgan totally nuts. It must be what this snotty Esmerelda kid had been doing...

Now Sean stepped back from his basket. "C'mon guys, let's play basketball!" He made a graceful layup, landing on the floor so hard the floorboards rattled.

There was a crashing sound from below, like someone had dropped about ten cast iron pots. "Jeez, it's Esmerelda," hissed Morgan. Then a clumping echoed on the stairs. "She's coming!"

Grasping his Nerf ball, Sean jumped experimentally on the floor. It rattled again, even louder this time. "What are you doing?" Morgan snatched the ball from him and threw it over her shoulder. "That mean Ezzie girl is going to get even madder at us!"

"Let's hide!" said Ronan. He loved practical jokes. "The closet!"

"How about the floor?" Sean said calmly. "Look!" He jumped again, and Morgan saw a small square of floorboards move. They'd been cut in a panel.

A trapdoor!

6

The Getaway

"Cool! Guys, help me open it!" Morgan pried up one corner of the floor panel and the boys scrambled to lift it. Ronan shone his flashlight into the darkness beneath the floor. "Doesn't look too bad," he said, clicking on his flashlight. "It's just a little cubbyhole." He slid down into it.

"Sean, you're next," said Morgan, and Sean slithered through the opening. Morgan quickly followed, and she and Sean slid the panel closed over their heads.

Morgan didn't hear the room door open, but she nearly jumped at the banging right over their heads, as if Ezzie was drumming her feet on the trapdoor. Morgan had to keep her mouth closed tight to keep from laughing. The boys were snickering through their hands.

"You brats think you can mock me?" yelled the girl. "But I will have the last laugh!" There was a clumping sound on the floor and down the stairs. Then silence.

"I can't wait to tell my mom about old Ezzie out there," Morgan whispered. "Talk about a wackadoodle!"

"What do we do now?" asked Sean.

"I wonder if there's another way out of here," Ronan whispered, and shone the light in all four directions.

Sean peered around the hole, following Ronan's little beam of light. "There's a door!"

As Sean patted one wall, Ronan pointed the light at it. Morgan saw another square cutout, about two and a half feet on each side, with leather hinges on one side. The door was fastened by a loop of cord around a nail in the adjacent wall. On his hands and knees, Sean reached out to open the panel. Ronan aimed the light into the darkness beyond.

"You won't believe this," Sean said. "Stairs!" He scooted past Ronan. "I'll go first—Ronan, you shine the flashlight over my head so I can see where I'm going."

Ronan stuck the flashlight in his mouth, holding it between his teeth. He crawled through the door, Morgan right behind him. "I can't believe we're doing this," she said. "It's like a movie!"

"It's great!" said Ronan through his clenched teeth.

Sean carefully put one foot on the first stair. "Watch it—the stairs are really steep."

Ronan took the flashlight out of his mouth, shining the beam downward past Sean to reveal a staircase.

"Let's go!" said Morgan. "But try to step lightly, okay? Or you-know-who will be after us!"

The boys tiptoed down about ten stairs, Morgan right behind them. They reached a landing the size of a picnic table, only to find another flight below. A pinprick of light barely showed at the end. "That's got to be the way out!" Morgan whispered.

They crept down the second set of stairs, toward a thin line of light. Was it a Hobbit-sized door opened partway? The stairs ended at a short passage lined with wood, hardly three feet high. Morgan and the boys dropped to their knees again, and scuttled toward what had to be the opening.

Morgan pushed cobwebs from her face and shuddered, trying not to think about how many spiders and other crawly things that had to be in this passageway. It had a funny smell too—salty and seaweedy, like the odor she'd detected last night, blowing into the restaurant from the river.

The tunnel ended not at a door, but a wooden board propped against a wall, leaving just enough space to allow a slit of light to come through. Morgan pushed on the board. It fell over, creating a space large enough for her and her cousins to slide through.

They emerged into a small wooden structure with a canvas floor, and Ronan turned off his flashlight. A shovel leaned against the wall next to the door, a rake was lying on the dingy wrinkled canvas, and more rumpled canvas was piled in one corner. A window of spotted glass was open, mildewed pink curtains flapping in the breeze. Sean crab-walked to the window, rising just high enough for his eyes to clear the window ledge. He peered outside. "We're in the garden shed that belongs to the bed-and-breakfast."

Morgan bent over and scooted to the window, beckoning to Ronan. "Come see." She and Ronan imitated Sean, peeking just over the window ledge back at the Victorian house. Something crashed upstairs. Through the opened window, a familiar voice floated down. "Blasted children!"

Morgan ducked her head, giggling, and the boys collapsed next to her, chortling. They couldn't stop, snorting with laughter until they were breathless. Morgan clutched her stomach, aching from laughing so hard. "Wasn't this getaway like, the best?"

"Awesome," Sean said solemnly.

"Yeah! Who knew we'd find a trapdoor *and* a secret staircase!" Ronan grinned so widely his eyes were all squinty.

Morgan gazed at her cousins, a surge of affection for them making her eyes smart. Sean and Ronan were her little guys—just like brothers, if she'd had any. Of course, they wouldn't *stay* her little guys—before long, they would be taller than she was, and have zits and loud voices and gigantic feet. They would probably make gross jokes too, like a lot of the boys at school.

Morgan knew she was changing too—and maybe she

would grow away from Sean and Ronan. She didn't want to, but it happens—you can't help growing up. Her summer was already booked with boating trips with her mom and dad, and camping with her friends and their families. Then a realization hit Morgan—what if this was the last time she and the boys would hang out together for two whole day?

Morgan knew what she had to do. Right now. She'd make this a weekend to remember! Show her little guys the Best. Time. Ever.

She needed to come up with something even more amazing than *The Goonies* anniversary events! But...what would it be?

"Let's do something...well, mind-blowing!" Morgan said suddenly. "Something so cool, so Astoria-ish, that everyone who went to *The Goonies'* celebration will wish they'd thought of it."

"But we just did it," said Sean. "We escaped from Esmerelda!"

Morgan had an idea. "Sean, I bet your map can help us come up with a totally awesome Astoria adventure." She patted her hoodie pocket, feeling around her sea lion candle for the map. It was gone! The paper must have slid out when they were crawling around that passage. Too bad you couldn't pay her to go back in there.

Well, at least one mystery was solved. Now she knew the tunnel was how the people Aunt Shannon had talked about had "mysteriously disappeared" from the B&B. Were these people cheapskates, and didn't want to pay for their room? Or...smugglers?

"Let's not tell anyone about the staircase or the passage—keep it our secret," Morgan told the boys. "We'll let people keep thinking it's a creepy old house." Just then, she remembered something else. The B&B owner had said she would be gone at the Anniversary events today, and locked up the house. She obviously let her grandkids have a free run of her B&B. But if this girl wasn't a granddaughter, then who was she?

There was a tinkling sound on the shed's roof, like a handful of pebbles hitting it. Morgan scooted back to the window, and saw ol' Ezzie was up in the tower room. She stood in front of the opened window, staring right at Morgan. The girl threw something out, which landed on top of the shed with a clang. As Morgan instinctively ducked, whatever Ezzie had tossed dropped off the roof into the weeds below the window.

Ronan jumped to his feet. "What the—"

"Ezzie's just trying to get attention," said Morgan. "I say we ignore her."

"Let's see what she wants," said Sean. He pulled on the curvy brass knob of the shed door. The door didn't move.

Ronan said, "I'll try." He turned the doorknob and yanked, but the door still didn't budge. "It's not locked, it's stuck."

Morgan jumped up too, ready to give the door a try.

Before she could, Sean boosted himself up and through the window. Morgan could hear some rustling around in the weeds, then the doorknob rattled.

"Ronan," Sean said through the door, "I'll push and you pull."

Morgan stood back, smiling. *Boys like jobs.*

Both boys grunted and strained, and finally the door creaked. Ronan stumbled backwards as the door swung open, Sean practically falling inside the shed. He held the metal measuring cup Valerie had used earlier. There was a piece of paper wrapped around it, attached with one of Morgan's purple elastic hair fasteners. "I think Ezzie's sending us a message."

He pulled off the elastic band and handed it to Morgan. Dropping the cup to the canvas floor, he opened the paper. There was a message all right, written in elegant, flowing cursive. Morgan read it aloud.

I have your map. If you would like it back in your possession, meet me in the house. I have a proposition for you. A business proposition.

Yours truly,

Letitia Lahti.

7

The Mystery Job

"I say we go inside," said Sean. "Find out what this proposition is."

"Yeah—she might pay us!" Ronan looked eagerly at Morgan and his brother. "The money could be really awesome—think how many more games we could play at the arcade!"

"Wait a minute." Morgan pushed the door partway shut. "Are you sure you want to get mixed up with this snarky chick? She can't be trusted." Morgan remembered brushing past the girl earlier. "She stole your map right out of my pocket!"

"It *is* a pretty great map," Sean admitted.

"Yeah, no wonder she wanted it," added Ronan. "Let's go before she changes her mind."

Morgan rolled her eyes and picked up the measuring cup. "Okay." *Giving the boys a good time means I've got to go along with what they want, right?*

The boys helped Morgan prop the board against the wall again, to conceal the opening they'd come through, and they trooped through the shed door. Catching a flash of red near the window, Morgan ignored it and trailed the boys to the back door, now unlocked. As they entered the kitchen, she set the cup on the counter and hollered, "Okay, we're here. What do you want?"

"Come up to the Tower Room," Ezzie called from upstairs.

The boys rushed up the stairs. Morgan followed more slowly. She didn't like the way this Ezzie-Letitia person was calling all the shots. In fact, she seemed like big trouble— why couldn't her cousins see it? As she entered Room Seven behind the boys, the girl was already settled on the window seat, her tatty dress spread out on the cushion. In the midday light, her light complexion seemed even paler. She held up Sean's opened map.

"You wrote on my map!" Sean looked balefully at the girl. "No one gets to write on my drawings."

"But I had to," the girl said in a coaxing voice. "I needed to mark all the places in Astoria I want you to go."

As Ronan studied the new markings on Sean's map, Morgan said, "Wait a second—your name's 'Letitia?'"

"I prefer Lottie," said the girl with a regal lift of her chin.

"Lottie Lahti.'" Morgan snickered. "What are you, a Marvel comic character?"

Lottie gave her a snooty look. Morgan focused on the

map, and saw Lottie had drawn several precise stars at various Astoria locales, with neatly executed arrows all over.

"Why do you want us to visit these places?" Morgan demanded.

"Why can't you go yourself?" Ronan asked.

"Why..." Lottie's eyes shifted as she set the map aside. "Because my mama is angry with me, and she and papa said I can't go anywhere."

"Mama?" Morgan repeated sarcastically. "Papa?' No one calls their parents that!" And where were her parents anyway?

Lottie ignored her, giving Sean a big, blue-eyed stare.

"You mean you're grounded?" asked Sean. "What did you do?"

"Grounded?" Lottie's brows drew together. "Mama is so upset she has vowed she's never going to let me out of the house!"

"You must have done something pretty bad," remarked Sean.

"Oh, come on, L.L.," said Morgan. "You can drop the acting. Just tell us, what you want, and why we should help you."

"Very well." Lottie reached behind her, and brought out a sheaf of papers. She took one sheet from the stack, showing it first to Sean, then Ronan, and finally, to Morgan.

It was some type of flyer or ad, written in the same flowing cursive as the first message, only the writing was much larger.

Young lady of good family seeks the whereabouts of one William "Billy" Smith, lately the cabin boy of the "Schooner Astoria Mist." Mr. Smith, if you see this advertisement, you may call upon Miss Letitia Lahti directly at The Lahti House, and collect the reward for services rendered.

Otherwise, any information about Mr. Smith would be greatly appreciated. He is approximately fourteen years of age, with shaggy chestnut hair and a fuzzy moustache, and has been seen with a red silk eyepatch over his left eye.

Anyone who has sighted Mr. Smith or has news of him may contact Miss Lahti at the aforementioned location. A modest reward will be given to the person or persons who provide information leading to the successful tracking down of Mr. Smith.

Below the text was a tiny, circular photo of a girl's face, obviously cut out from the B&B brochure. "That's me, right there," Lottie preened. "My advertisement is very well done, wouldn't you say?"

"You are some piece of work!" Morgan snatched the flyer and tossed it on the floor. "You're the one who messed up all Valerie's brochures! No wonder your 'mama' is mad at you!"

"Never mind that," said Lottie. "I—"

"What's 'chestnut' hair?" asked Ronan.

"Auburn," said Lottie.

"What's auburn?" Ronan wanted to know.

"Reddish," Morgan said impatiently. "Now—"

"What's 'services rendered'?"

"Doing something nice!" Morgan burst out. "Can we just—"

"Be quiet!" said Lottie. "We must settle the business at hand—"

"Who made you the queen of the world?" Morgan asked, seething. "We don't have to obey you—"

"As I was saying," interrupted Lottie, "I would like to engage you to place my advertisement around Astoria, at the locations I've marked. And do post it in the order and routes I've indicated on the map."

"*My* map," said Sean. He grabbed his map from the cushion, spreading it out. Morgan now saw that next to each star was a number.

"It's a very fine map," said Lottie in a suck-up kind of voice. "In fact, your map will be crucial to the success of my venture."

"If we do it, will you pay us?" Ronan said.

"Indeed I shall." Lottie rose from the window seat and tossed the seat cushion aside. She lifted the wooden seat to reveal a roomy storage space. Leaning in, she drew out a drawstring bag of royal blue velvet that clinked as she moved it. Lottie loosened the cords, slid her fingers inside and drew out three silver coins. Snapping the bag closed, she showed the coins to Morgan and the boys.

Ronan glanced at the coins then stuck out his chin. "If we hike all over Astoria for your ad, you're going to give us each one arcade token? I don't think so."

"They're not tokens," said Sean.

"They're silver dollars," Morgan said at the same time. "My grandpa once showed me a few of them."

Lottie tapped one foot impatiently. "Can we get on with this?"

"A dollar isn't that much more than a token," said Ronan.

Morgan peered closely at the coins. The dates on them were over one hundred years old, just like her grandpa's. "Actually, those coins are worth lots more than a dollar," Morgan said. "You could have a collector check their value—"

"Hold up one minute, Lottie-Lotto," Ronan broke in. "You've got more money in that bag, so you can pay us a *lot* more."

"That money is for Mr. Smith. Mama was saving it for her idea of a proper education—finishing school." Lottie's lip curled again in scorn. "But Bi—I mean, Mr. Smith deserves it much more."

"What's finishing school?" Sean asked.

"The worst place in the world!" said Lottie dramatically. "In any event, I cannot pay you anything more."

"I dunno—I'd do the job for the one silver dollar," said Sean. "But I don't know how we can do it—we're supposed to stay here until my mom and aunt show up."

"Sometimes you have to bend the rules," said Lottie, holding up one elegant finger. "And one more thing. You will need to provide proof that you have reached every starred location. So I will require you to bring back some kind of ticket or other small article from each place."

"You *require?*" said Morgan, incredulous.

"Like a...a scavenger hunt?" Sean said at the same time.

"Huh," said Ronan. "Seems like for one buck we can do the job any way we like. But how will we know what to bring you?"

"I'm sure you'll come up with something." Lottie seemed to allow herself a tiny smile. "But you need to depart right away. This job absolutely must be done by six o'clock sharp."

8

Almost Famous

Morgan folded her arms across her chest. "What are we, your stinkin' servants?" She was *so* ready to tell Lottie to stuff it. Especially since this kid clearly thought she could wrap the boys—*Morgan's* little guys—around her pinky finger! She stared at Lottie for a long moment. "I've got some questions first," said Morgan. "There's a lot that doesn't add up here. Such as, you obviously knew all about the cubby under the floor and the secret staircase."

"I should say I do—I know every nook and cranny of this house," said Lottie. "And I helped my papa build the stairs."

Yeah, sure, Morgan thought. *Okay, I'll play along.* "So why didn't you come right after us when we snuck away from you—"

"I've got a question too," Sean interrupted. "If you wanted to talk to us, and you knew all about the stairs and where they ended in the shed, why didn't you just meet us there?"

"Yeah," added Ronan. He pulled his Astoria legends guidebook from his back jeans pocket and opened it. "Instead of throwing beans and that stupid cup to get our attention, then making us come back to the house."

Lottie's face turned an odd color. Sort of...grayish. "I told you, I'm not allowed to leave the house."

Ronan grabbed the pen he'd stuck inside the book cover and scribbled something on a page.

"Ronan," said his brother, "you're not supposed to write in books."

"This book isn't from the library. Mom bought it for me." Ronan pocketed his book then narrowed his eyes at Lottie. "You don't look so good. Are you sick or something?"

"Yeah, it's like you look kind of white around the edges," said Sean.

"It's not polite to make personal comments about someone's appearance," Lottie said primly. She looked down at her pale skin of her forearm, lifting up her lacy sleeve. "But since you did, the fact is, my grandparents came from Finland," she said. "We Finns are very fair."

"You're not fair at all," said Ronan, "if you're asking us to run all over Astoria for one measly coin."

"'Fair' also means blond," Sean said unexpectedly. "By the way, who's Billy? Your boyfr—"

"Mr. Smith is none of your concern," said Lottie. "You have his description, and that's all you need to know."

"I'm not done with my questions," Morgan said, ticked

off at the way Lottie had snubbed Sean. "Back to the secret staircase—why did you and your dad build it anyway?"

"Mama wanted a grand house," Lottie said promptly. "Our family moved in when the house was only half finished. The staircase was part of the unfinished part. Of course it had to be sealed away, for safety reasons."

"Of course," Morgan mimicked. "So...you helped your dad with the house? I highly doubt that! You don't look the type—"

"You're wrong!" Lottie clenched her fists. "I did help him—I loved working with Papa!" She seemed to go paler. "He was going to help me study to be an architect, and I would be famous—a lady architect!"

"If you want to be famous, all you have to do is post a bunch of videos on YouTube," Ronan pointed out.

Lottie looked baffled. "What's a 'you tube?' You speak very oddly, I must say."

"Oh, come on," said Morgan. "Can we cut the—"

"Never mind the tubes," Lottie interrupted. "I was determined to give everything to my studies, and I just *knew* my designs would be in great demand! But Mama—" An even fiercer look crossed her face.

"What about your mom?" Morgan asked curiously.

"She didn't want her daughter to be an architect, or learn the building trade. In fact, she forbade me to study my papa's architectural books, and told Papa he would have to get along without my help. I told her that I was grown up enough to make this decision, but she said I was still a little girl!"

Morgan felt the first stirrings of sympathy for Lottie. Wasn't she stuck at this B&B because her mom was treating her like a kid too? "What happened then?"

"I'll tell you what happened," said Lottie, fire in her eyes. "I was so angry I ran away fr—" She broke off.

"You ran away from home?" Sean's eyes rounded.

Lottie paused, then gave a short laugh. "What would my mama say? Besides, what kind of young lady would do *that?*"

Someone who wanted something badly? thought Morgan. "So why didn't your dad finish the other half of the house? Or hire someone else to help build it?"

Lottie looked away for a moment. "Papa was quite occupied, working on other buildings in town," she finally said. "So he didn't have time to complete our house without my help." Her voice seemed to catch. "Once he'd finished the other jobs, it's my...understanding that he didn't have the heart to keep working on the house."

"You've got an explanation for everything, don't you?" said Morgan.

Lottie only sighed. "Fame, it would seem, would be out of my reach. I am instead determined not to be...forgotten."

Morgan continued to stare at Lottie. This twerp was pretty fantastic about staying in character. But just what was the deal here? For some reason, this girl's crazy scavenger hunt job had to take place all over town. And the job had to be done *today*—the biggest day of *The Goonies* Anniversary Celebration—

A light went on in her head.

"Okay, I get it!" Morgan started to laugh. "This whole posting ads deal is some kind of huge joke, right? A publicity stunt for the Anniversary Celebration!"

Lottie wrinkled her pale forehead. "What are you talking about?"

"Or wait—it's to promote the Lahti B&B!" As Sean and Ronan exchanged puzzled looks, Morgan laughed harder. "You want to be famous, huh? You'll get tons of attention with all the people here for the Anniversary—Jeez, I've really got to hand it to you!"

Valerie the B&B owner was obviously in on the scam too. In fact, she and Lottie probably cooked up the scheme together. It was off the charts amazing, the way Valerie had pretended being upset about her brochures being ruined, and the B&B not getting customers!

Finally Morgan caught her breath. Well, if Lottie and Valerie had gone to all this trouble, why spoil their plans? And hey—this wacky scavenger hunt could be the Big Astoria Adventure she'd give the boys!

"Okay, guys, I've changed my mind," Morgan faced the boys, her mouth curving in a cheeky grin. "I say let's go for it!"

"You'll do it?" Lottie looked so pleased Morgan could

swear she had a glow surrounding her. Wait...not really a glow. A strange, grayish-white aura...

"That's what we said, Lotto," Ronan told her. "We'll take the job."

Sean grinned. "Awesome!"

"We'll even do it for one silver dollar," said Ronan resignedly, but his eyes were shining.

Lottie rose, and with a regal gesture she handed Sean her stack of flyers. "You seem the most trustworthy," she said to him. "Before you leave, you'll need something to afix my advertisement. In the kitchen, I will set out..." she frowned, "...it's not glue, but some sticky material I found. Scottish tape, I believe it's called."

"You mean, Scotch tape," said Sean.

"Yes, you may use that," said Lottie, still acting like *she* was doing them a favor, instead of the other way around. "I will see you back here at six sharp. If you don't have a pocket watch, you'll know it's six when the moon sets."

Morgan wrinkled her forehead. *Pocket watch?* She took out her phone, waving it at Lottie. "I'll be able to keep track of time."

Lottie only stared at the phone, as if mesmerized. "What on earth is that?"

"It's a—" Morgan broke off, exasperated. She wouldn't give Lottie the satisfaction of explaining the obvious, playing along with this scheme of hers.

Lottie seemed to drag her gaze away from the phone with an effort. "And don't forget to bring your items of proof." She paused, as if she expected Morgan to curtsy or some other not-gonna-happen thing.

Morgan only said, "Okay, see ya. We'll leave as soon as I call my mom."

As Lottie sashayed from the room, Morgan remembered the contest. "Guys...you realize that if we do this job, you probably won't have time to fill out your contest entry for the Café. It's due by six too."

"Sure we will," Ronan said confidently. He pulled out his Astoria legends book again, opening it to show Morgan a multi-folded piece of paper. "Got the entry form right here." He crammed the book and form back in his pocket. "I'll have all afternoon to come up with a great story while we're running around town."

"If you say so." Morgan pressed her mom's number on her phone. Now, all she had to do was get permission from her mom and Aunt Shannon, for her and the boys to wander all over Astoria without a grownup.

Which was about as likely as Morgan giving Lotto Girl a curtsy.

"Mom, we ran out of things to do here," Morgan said into her phone, her eyes on the boys. "We were thinking of heading back to the arcade."

Just before Morgan had pressed her mom's number, she had warned the boys, "We might have to...um, pretend a little, to do this scavenger hunt."

"You mean, say we're doing one thing, but doing something else," Ronan summed up.

"Guys, that's lying," Sean said, looking unhappy.

"Maybe we do have to...well, *deceive* our moms a little," Morgan had said carefully, "but it's for a good cause." Well, it was! They could help Valerie make the B&B a success, or help Lotto Girl get paid for her acting gig. Or whatever. "Let me give it a try."

Now Morgan focused on her mom's voice. "Morgan," her mom was saying, "I don't like the idea of you three going to the arcade by yourselves..." Her mom's voice was barely audible with all the noise going on at the event they were attending. Someone was talking over a loudspeaker, the mic reverberating, punctuated by cheers and hoots of laughter.

"Why not?" Morgan said. "The arcade is only a quick walk away. Same as the Oregon Film Museum. Could we go there too?"

"Let me grab your aunt, see what she thinks. Hang on."

Morgan looked over at her cousins, lolling on the bed looking at Sean's map. Ronan consulted his book, showing his brother some pages, then Sean pulled out a pen and scribbled what looked to be more arrows and notations on the map.

From the phone, Morgan heard her mom murmur something, then her aunt said, "Nicky, there are crossing guards at the busiest intersections, and museum guides on every block. The town's never been safer for kids."

"But Shannon—"

"Let's not treat our children like babies," her aunt said. "Be right back—I'm just going to look at those souvenirs."

"Morgan." Mom came back on the line. "Go ahead, honey. We're fine with the arcade and the Film Museum."

"What if we get...um, hungry?" Morgan said, and crossed her fingers. "Would it be okay if we leave the arcade to go...somewhere else for a snack?"

There was a long pause. Finally her mom said, "Sweetie." She sounded funny. "Be honest—do you guys want to leave the B&B because you're...uncomfortable there?"

"Why would we be uncomfortable?" Feeling guilty, Morgan glanced at her cousins again. Sean was packing his Nerf ball and the stack of flyers into his backpack, while Ronan slipped his flashlight next to the pen in his shirt pocket. They were clearly up for this scavenger hunt adventure...

"Well..." Mom lowered her voice. "Something came to me after we left the B&B. It's not like me at all, but..." she hesitated. "When I was lying in bed this morning, I had the strangest feeling of being...watched."

"Mom, that's just...silly," said Morgan, but her pulse

picked up speed. She couldn't tell her mom she'd felt the exact same way.

"I guess it is," said Mom. "But after having that strange feeling, *then* hearing about the earthquake and the skeleton being stolen—it just seems...oh, forget it. Maybe I'm the one with the overactive imagination, not your aunt. Anyway, here she comes. You've got plenty of money for the arcade?"

"Yeah," said Morgan. "I'll give the boys a good time."

"Of course you will," said her mom. "The breeze is a bit chilly, so have the boys bring a jacket. And promise me you'll stick together, not matter what."

"I promise," said Morgan. She aimed her phone away from her mouth. "Guys, pack your jackets too."

"Thanks, hon," said her mom. "We're trusting you to take good care of your cousins."

"I will," said Morgan, watching Ronan tie his windbreaker to the straps of his backpack. Ready to say "Bye" and end the call, she caught Sean giving her a mildly reproachful look. They would be breaking a *lot* of rules to do this job for Lottie. "Say Mom," she said, trying to be as honest as she could. "Just so you know, we'll probably take the...long way to the arcade."

9

The Hunt is On

"When you said the 'long way' to the arcade," said Ronan, breathing hard, "You weren't kidding."

At the open-air top of the Astoria Column, Morgan hung onto the metal railing to catch her breath, Sean leaning next to her. After the punishing hike up Coxcomb Hill, Astoria's steepest—and given all the hills in town, that was saying something—Sean had found a shortcut to the Column. Morgan bought three tickets, stowing them carefully in her jeans pocket. Then they started up the umpteen hundred stairs to climb the 125 foot-high Column, Lottie's #1 location on the map. And finally, here they were.

Gazing toward the river, Morgan could see the town buzzing with cars and tourists, the noise of *The Goonies'* Anniversary activities drifting up the hill. Although they had permission to go to the Film Museum, Morgan would have to make sure she and the boys steered clear of any other Anniversary events. She couldn't risk running into her mom and aunt. "Okay, Sean, we'd better get that ad posted."

Ronan took a flyer from his brother's backpack. From his pocket, Sean extracted the roll of tape Lottie had left out for them. He tore off about a foot of tape and attached the paper to the nearest wall. "It can get windy up here," he said.

Morgan watched, hiding her misgivings. This flyer— and all the rest of them—would probably get torn down by some visitor or another within a few minutes, either for a souvenir, or just to be mean. But since Lottie didn't seem inclined to get her queenly self to the Column or around town, she'd never know her flyers would be seen for maybe three minutes. If at all.

"Come on, we don't have all day," said Ronan, as Sean added extra tape to the corners. "Don't we have at least five more places to go?"

"Yeah," said Morgan, and checked the time on her phone. "There's another long walk down that humungous hill. And we only have a few hours—"

She broke off as a young teenage guy in a pirate-y looking outfit rushed clumsily up the stairs. He wore a white shirt with a high collar, a loose black sport jacket and scuffed boots. A red kerchief covered his head, and round sunglasses were slipping down his nose. Morgan couldn't help noticing that he didn't seem winded at all by the climb, which was kind of unusual. Maybe he ran marathons or something—

"Finished!" Sean jammed the tape back into his pocket. He bolted down the stairs past the teen, calling over his shoulder. "Last one down is a rotten egg!"

Morgan forgot about the pirate guy as they left the grounds of the Column. Heading downhill, Ronan and Sean picked up their pace, and before long they were half a block ahead of her. "Guys!" Morgan called. "We're supposed to stay together!"

The boys stopped to let her catch up. Once downtown, Morgan, Sean and Ronan threaded their way through the crowds. Rounding the corner from the Green Griddle Bakery, they arrived at the replica of Fort Astoria, the #2 location on the map. Sean began prowling around the small wooden stockade for a likely posting spot. "There's no ticket to buy here," Morgan pointed out. "What'll we do for ol' Lotto's proof?"

"Lemme think." Ronan examined the colorful mural of a frontiersman holding a musket, with some Native Americans nearby, then gazed around the grounds, filled with flowerbeds. "I bet my mom would like it here, with the history and all. I wonder if any of the ghost-hunting shows she likes have checked out this little fort?"

"I think they go for spookier places," said Sean, taping

the flyer to the back side of the wood structure. "Now what can we come up with to prove we were here?"

"We could pick a flower," Morgan said, "but someone would probably see us and get us into trouble." *Posting a flyer is enough of a risk.*

"Yeah," said Ronan, running his hand over the old logs. Quickly looking around to see if they were being watched, he inspected a section of rough wood and picked off some long splinters. As Sean pulled out another length of tape, Ronan stuck the shreds of wood to it. "The splinters were an inspired idea," said Morgan as they left the grounds. "You guys are a great team."

"Where to next?" Ronan asked as they walked past a small gated garden.

Sean consulted the map. "The old jail."

"You mean the Oregon Film Museum," said Morgan. Lottie had marked the museum as #3 on Sean's map. "Did you know the movie *Overboard* was filmed around Astoria too?" It was another one of her mom's favorites, and she'd made Morgan watch it with her a gazillion times. "The star of *Overboard* acted a lot like Lottie, all snobby and bossy, like she was better than everybody else," Morgan said. "That lady got what she deserved, falling off the boat in the movie."

Lottie could use a good dunking, too, to help her get rid of that attitude.

"Can you believe Lottie-Lotto tried to fake us out, that

she hadn't heard of YouTube?" said Ronan as they approached the museum. "Everyone knows about YouTube!"

"Yeah, unless they've been living under a rock." Morgan laughed.

"Or in a cave," said Sean.

"Lottie put on such a good act," said Morgan, "that if she was in a movie, she could win a Best Actress Oscar, for sure!"

As she and the boys wound their way through about fifty people in the parking lot out front, she gave the Museum a once-over. It was a square building of gray stone, and just below the roofline read, *County Jail, 1914-1976*. At the entrance, Morgan sighed regretfully as she bought their tickets. "Too bad we don't have time to look inside after we paid for admission," she muttered, trailing after the boys.

She and Sean searched the outside of building for the best spot for the flyer, as Ronan peeked in the barred windows. "I wonder if any crooks or desperados died in there," he said. "The ghost hunters should try this place—it's definitely creepier than Fort Astoria."

Luckily, the place was so crowded with Anniversary visitors that nobody noticed when Sean posted the ad right under a plastic head of "Sloth," perched next to the front door. As they turned to go, Morgan looked curiously at a young teen slouched on the other side of the entry, one hand shading his eyes, a ferocious scowl on his face.

Red kerchief, round sunglasses, pirate getup. The boy
they'd seen at the top of the Column.

Morgan and her cousins waited next to the train tracks
on the south end of Astoria's Riverwalk, watching for the
old-fashioned trolley to take them to the Columbia River
Maritime Museum. It wasn't *that* far to walk, but after
hiking up to the Column then across downtown, Morgan
and Ronan were ready for a rest.

Not Sean. He was shooting imaginary lay-ups with his
Nerf ball. Ronan watched him for a minute, then pulled out
his guidebook. "I found more cool smuggling stories in my
book," he said. He studied a couple of pages, and added
more scribbles. "And I got more ideas about the contest. I
think the skeleton had to be a smuggler."

"Why?" asked Morgan, checking the time on her phone
again.

"Well, duh," said Ronan. "Who else would be down in a
dark hole or tunnel next to where ships dock?"

"Good point," said Morgan. As the dark green and
maroon trolley approached, the bell chiming, Morgan
added, "Hey, Sean—pack your Nerfball. Here comes our
ride."

They climbed aboard, bought their tickets from the
smiling conductor, and squirmed through the nearly full
trolley car to the back.

"Man, people sure take the Anniversary Celebration seriously," said Morgan. "Have you ever seen so many goofball costumes?" Besides all the pirates, some trolley riders were dressed in a mash-up of *The Goonies*' characters.

"Sean, I know the trolley isn't on our map of places to post the flyer," Ronan said, "but maybe Lotto will pay us extra if we leave a flyer with the conductor."

"Good idea," said Sean. He rose and wormed his way to the front of the car. Morgan saw him show the flyer to the kindly-looking gray-haired woman. She smiled, then took the flyer and set it on the train console.

As Sean turned around, an odd expression came over his face. He headed back to their seat.

"Let's not forget to tell Lotto to come up with more cash," Ronan said.

"I just saw something kind of...funny," Sean said slowly. "There's a teenager up front I think we saw before."

"So?" said Ronan.

"Astoria is a small town," Morgan pointed out. "We're bound to see some of the same people again."

"But I think it's the guy who was on the Column stairs just as we were leaving. He's got a red cloth on his head and sunglasses."

"Guys," said Morgan, a jittery feeling in her stomach, "I didn't mention it, but I saw him at...the Film Museum too."

"Do you think he's...following us?" asked Ronan.

"Of course not," Morgan said quickly, not wanting to worry the boys. "This guy has got to be another fanboy of *The Goonies*."

"Okay, maybe it's just a coincidence," Sean said. "If he's not dressing up for the Anniversary, he's got to be one of the characters in the *Shanghaied in Astoria* play. Like Lottie."

Morgan shifted uneasily. They never *had* gotten Lottie to admit she was an actress, but Morgan didn't want to remind Sean of *that.*

Sean fiddled with his backpack fastening. "You've got to admit it's pretty strange that we came here straight from the Film Museum, but this boy was already on the trolley, ahead of us. Either he knows a shortcut, or..." he shrugged.

Ronan's eyes widened. As he stared at the front of the trolley, the teenager turned around, his dark glasses glinting in their direction. The butterflies in Morgan's stomach started fluttering like crazy. *The boy was already on the trolley...Like he knew where we were going next...*

The Maritime Museum on the waterfront was nearly deserted, for a Saturday. With that fanboy teenager turning up a little too frequently, Morgan would have felt safer if there had been more of a crowd here. A few people were taking photos of the ginormous ship's anchor in the center of the Museum courtyard, and another couple was strolling toward the paddlewheeler cruise boat, *The Princess Columbia*, in port beyond the courtyard. The ship's gangway stretched onto the dock, and a man holding a clipboard stood nearby, clearly to keep trespassers from boarding. But with no official Anniversary event here, Morgan guessed most celebrators were downtown, on the other side of Marine Drive.

As Morgan bought the Museum tickets they wouldn't use, Ronan acted as lookout while Sean posted the flyer. He chose a spot near the main doors, next to a poster advertising a local concert. "I wish we had time to go inside," he said as Morgan joined them.

She checked the time on her phone. "It's already four o'clock...but maybe we can stay for a couple of minutes."

Sean ambled around the corner of the building, Morgan and Ronan following him. He stopped at the front glass wall, where a Coast Guard boat was displayed inside. Bow pointed sharply upward, the cutter was fixed onto a high fake wave, like it was caught in a storm. Four dummy "sailors" manned the craft.

"Wouldn't it be exciting, to be on a boat in a storm like that?" Sean said wistfully.

"That's nothing," said a growly voice behind them.

Morgan nearly jumped. She whirled around to find the pirate boy standing a short distance away. Even sunglasses, he was squinting against the late afternoon sunlight.

Morgan lifted her chin. "What do you mean?" Now she knew it for sure—this boy *was* following them. A *stalker.*

"Yeah, what are you talking about?" said Ronan, a pugnacious look on his face.

"I've been in the worst storms on the Columbia," the boy said disdainfully. "So fierce we had to lash ourselves to the mast to stay on deck."

"Ahoy, matey, I'm sure you have," said Morgan, dripping sarcasm. "You and Captain Hook and the rest of his Merry Men."

"Merry Men go with Robin Hood," Sean corrected. "Peter Pan has the Lost Boys." He looked at the teen. "What are you, a real-life pirate?" he asked. Her cousin could be kind of gullible.

"Something like that," said the teen. He adjusted his glasses, then reached in his black coat pocket and pulled out a long, thin cigar. From another pocket, he produced a box of matches.

Sean gave him a disapproving look. "You're not supposed to smoke here—didn't you see the sign? 'Do not smoke within 25 feet of this building.'"

"I do what I like." The boy struck the match, but nothing happened.

"You're too young to smoke anyway," Ronan said.

"No I'm not!" the boy struck the match again, but still nothing. "The blasted damp," he muttered.

Morgan frowned. Hadn't Lottie said *blasted* too?

"Maybe your match is pretend," said Ronan.

"Like you," Morgan added, but she felt another nervous twinge in her stomach.

"I'll bet you wish you were me!" said the boy, throwing his box of matches onto the pavement.

"You're littering too," said Sean, and bent to pick up the small box.

"I get to travel the world!" The teen took a halting step toward them. "And make a lot of money!"

"In your imagination, maybe," said Ronan. "You're too cool for school?"

"I don't go to school," the boy said, a menacing look on his face. "And you'd better watch what you say. I saw your paper at the new jail—what do you know about her anyway?"

"Her who?" asked Morgan, playing dumb.

"You know who! The girl in the advertisement. Miss Letitia Lahti."

10

Pursued

"Lottie?" Sean reached around for his backpack and drew out another flyer. "She—"

The teen snatched the paper, drawing it close to his eyes. Then he thrust the ad in Morgan's face. "That's her writing!"

"We're just doing a job!" Morgan broke in, feeling even more uneasy. This kid was turning from a nuisance to maybe...dangerous? "How'd you find us?"

The boy looked scornful. "I saw you around the shed at the Lahti place. It was easy to track you around town—but what were you doing at her house?"

"None of your business!" said Morgan. "Now just go away."

"Make me," said the teen, carefully holding the paper.

"Quit following us," Morgan said, "Or we'll...we'll call the police!"

"Police?" The boy sneered. "You think I'm scared of them? I told you, I do whatever I want."

Out of the corner of her eye, Morgan saw Ronan sidle away toward the courtyard. Maybe he had a plan for getting away from this guy? She kept talking to the teen, so he wouldn't notice Ronan leaving. "Sure you do," she said. "Right up until the police put you in juvenile detention."

Sean crossed his arms. "Yeah, they'll call your mother and then you'll really be in trouble." He passed the box of matches to Morgan. "Speaking of, Mom wouldn't want me to have these."

As Morgan pocketed the matches, the teen's face changed. "I don't have a mother," he said shortly. "Or a father."

Morgan felt a jolt of pity, then realized this stalker guy was probably lying. "Oh, come on."

"Who takes care of you then?" Sean obviously didn't realize they were dealing with a *serious* troublemaker.

"Never mind that!" The boy waved the paper at Morgan again. "You haven't answered me—what do you know about Letitia?" He crowded closer, as if to trap her and Sean against the building. "And where'd you get this advertisement?"

Weighing their options, Morgan's stomach began roiling with anxiety. The Museum courtyard had only a few people in it, and she heard some dogs yipping in the distance. But there was absolutely no one close by, and the main road was some distance away...

She looked around. Should she call for help? The dogs

were getting louder—would they drown out the sound of her voice? Then she saw Ronan—he was climbing the giant anchor in the middle of the courtyard! Oh, Jeez, did her mischievous cousin have to pick *now* to pull one of his tricks?

Ronan nimbly grasped the anchor's chain links to help him upward. At the top, he wound his legs around the anchor, waving at her with a triumphant grin on his face.

Poised to dash over and make him climb down, before he got them into bigger trouble than they were in already, she froze. What if they ran, but the teen followed them? Where could they go? As she watched her cousin, Ronan beckoned and pointed toward the river.

Morgan gave a tiny nod. He did have a plan. She squared her chin and stepped around the teen, grasping Sean's arm with one hand and grabbing the ad from the boy with the other. Crumpling up the paper, she said to Sean, "Get to the anchor!"

She threw the ad in the boy's face and she and Sean bolted away. She looked behind her to see the boy wobbling on the pavement, like he'd lost his balance. From a piece of paper in his face? As she and Sean neared the anchor, Ronan pulled up his legs, as if ready to jump. Morgan's alarm went into overdrive. "Don't, Ronan! It's at least ten feet high—"

"I can do it," Ronan called back. "See?" He leaped from the top, the windbreaker he'd tied to his backpack forming a small parachute, slowing his descent. He landed on both feet, grinning. "How about that?"

"Whoa," said Morgan, so impressed that for a second she forgot the problem teen. Sean said something, but all Morgan could hear were the yipping dogs. "What did you say?"

"He's coming after us!"

"This way!" said Ronan, and raced for the docks.

Morgan glanced over her shoulder, and saw the boy stumbling toward the courtyard. He wasn't moving very fast, but right here at the river's edge, with water all three sides, she, Ronan and Sean didn't have anywhere to run to...They would be trapped!

Despite her doubts, Morgan took off after Ronan, Sean at her heels. "Where are we going?" she panted. "We're not going to jump in the river to get away from him!"

"Nope," said Ronan, heading for the paddlewheeler. "Trust me."

He stopped a short distance from the guy with the clipboard, who'd moved away from the head of the gangway. The man was arguing with an older lady with a small mountain of luggage piled next to her. She held four toy poodles on two double leashes, straining on their tethers. "Ma'am, you can't take these dogs on board," he was saying, looking annoyed.

"I don't go anywhere without my little darlins'," the lady said stubbornly, the hyper poodles pacing frantically alongside her. As two of the dogs began jumping on the clipboard guy, their yapping was hurting Morgan's ears. "You'll be good on the ship, won't you, my lovie-dovies?" she cooed.

Ronan began tiptoeing in a wide circle around the twosome and the dogs, gesturing to Morgan and Sean to do the same.

The man didn't seem to notice them. "The passenger agreement is quite clear about pets, no matter how lovey-dovey they are," he said to the woman, frowning as he tried to shake his legs free. He pulled a cell phone from his pocket. "No exceptions. And since we depart within the hour—"

"You can make my darlins' a first," said the lady, loosening the dogs' leashes. As the dogs swarmed around the man, he tripped and fell to the wood dock. With the guy momentarily out of commission, Ronan snuck onto the gangway, Morgan and Sean creeping right behind him. They ran onto the paddlewheeler and crawled behind a row of deck chairs.

"You saved the day!" Morgan whispered. "But...what do we do now?" She peered around a chair to see the stalker boy wandering around the Museum courtyard. He stopped, looking confused, and adjusted his sunglasses. "He's still there."

"We can't stay too long on this ship," Sean murmured. "You heard the guy—it's leaving soon."

Morgan closed her eyes in frustration. She could only imagine the grounding that would await her if she and the boys got caught as stowaways on a cruise ship! Opening her eyes, she said, "Guys, we need a new plan."

Ronan peeked around the chair he was hiding behind. "Wait—I think the boy's given up. See?"

Morgan looked at the courtyard again. She saw the teen heading uncertainly for Marine Drive, stepping right into the flow the traffic as if the cars weren't even there. She gasped as one car, then another, missed him by inches, but he didn't seem to notice.

She kept watching, worried that a car would hit him. Even stalkers didn't deserve to be killed in traffic! But miraculously, he made his way across the busy road without mishap. Morgan's heart beat faster as he disappeared into the crowds walking toward the Armory building. *Something isn't adding up here—*

Sean elbowed her. "Look," he whispered, pointing toward the dock. An official looking woman in a crisp uniform, probably the captain, was talking sternly to Poodle Lady and waving some papers at her. The clipboard guy was brushing himself off. "It's our one chance to sneak off the boat."

"I say let's go for it," said Morgan, edging out from behind the chair.

"'Kay, on the count of three, we run as fast as we can," said Sean. "One...two...three!"

All together, they burst from behind the chairs and raced to the only escape route. Tearing down the gangway, they sprinted across the pier. "Wait!" an angry woman's voice called. "You kids have trespassed! I'm calling the police—"

"Keep running, guys!" Morgan gulped for air. "And don't look back."

11

Creeped Out at the Theatre

As her lungs felt ready to burst, Morgan raced two blocks to the Dratted Cat Bistro, the boys pounding the pavement next to her. Rounding the corner, she drew to a stop. "That was..." she wheezed, "way too close."

She turned to the boys. They were grinning at each other. "Way to go!" Sean lifted his palm to his brother.

"Yeah!" said Ronan, high-fiving Sean. "That was the funnest thing I ever did."

"The most fun," corrected Sean, then to Morgan, "Wasn't it *great?*"

"Better than great," Ronan gloated. "Awe-*some*! We really fooled that pirate dude, and those cruise people too."

"Yeah!" said Sean and pumped the air with his fist.

"You guys have got to be kidding!" Morgan said, exasperated. "That teenager was threatening us! And *we* could have been the ones hauled into juvenile detention!"

"But we got away, didn't we?" Sean said reasonably.

"That's not the point!" Morgan had had enough of this wacky scavenger hunt. What if she had put the boys in danger, all because she was mad at her mom about not being invited to the Anniversary Celebration? "Guys, I say we go back to the B&B."

"We haven't finished Lottie's job," said Sean.

"Yeah, and we only have one more place to go," Ronan said.

"But what if our moms find out what we've been up to? Morgan thought again of the teen crossing the busy main road. Her eyes were definitely playing tricks on her, because it looked like the cars had been...well, driving *right through him*... She swallowed nervously. "Really, we don't need those silver dollars—"

"We're not doing this for the money anyway," said Sean.

"Yeah, we're doing it for the fun!" added Ronan. "So let's get going and finish the job before we run out of time!"

Morgan took a deep breath. Having a day filled with skeletons, earthquakes, and a fake-o pirate guy following them, she was letting her imagination run away with her. Like her mom's had. Only she couldn't let the boys down, after she'd vowed to show her little guys a great adventure...

"All right—let's get to the theatre, and make it fast," Morgan said. "Our moms will kill us if we're not at the B&B when they get there."

The Freedom Theatre was a shabby, antique building with ornate stone carvings above the marquee. Ronan stared up at the big sign overhead. "*The Goonies* Playing All Day,'" he read, and flipped through his guidebook. "It says here this place was built in 1905."

"And made for 1905-sized crowds," Morgan muttered, glancing at the crowd spilling onto the street. "Getting in and out of here may be tricky," she said as they got in line to buy a ticket for the movie they wouldn't have time to see. "There must be hundreds of people here."

"Look, there are so many they had to set up Port-a-Potties." Ronan giggled and pointed to the side of the building.

Oh Jeez, thought Morgan. Boys did love potty stuff. "The bathrooms are probably too small for so many people."

Sean consulted his map again. "Lottie's got all kinds of marks and arrows here at the Theatre. I can hardly figure them out."

Ronan peered over his brother's shoulder. "It looks like we're supposed to go downstairs. To the basement."

"Wait a minute—" Morgan was *so* not up for the lowest floor of this decrepit old place. Surrounded by all these crazy fans, their voices deafening, she was feeling hemmed in too. What did they call that? Claustrophobic. "Let's just post the flyer out front here and head back to the B&B."

"We can't do that," Sean objected. "We have to do the job

right. So if we're supposed to go to the basement, that's where we have to go."

After a long wait in line, Ronan scribbling in his book the whole time, Morgan got their tickets. Sean squeezed through the crush of people to look around the foyer, covered with threadbare red carpet, while she and Ronan waited by one wall. He was back in a moment. "There's a stairway over there," and Sean pointed to a shadowy corner of the lobby. An exit sign stuck out from the wall, but it wasn't lit up in the customary red light.

Morgan sighed. "Aw, guys—"

"I'll bet it's spooky down there," Ronan said, his eyes lighting in anticipation. "Let's go." He led the way to the corner.

Morgan dragged her feet, grumbling to herself as they descended the stairs. *Why did I agree to this stupid scavenger hunt? Here I've spent two months' allowance on tickets to every landmark in Astoria, only Lottie will be paying us a silver dollar, which is basically squat! And after we had some wacko dude stalking us, here we are at this spooky old place, when I'd much rather be hanging out at the B&B! And worst of all, if Mom finds out about this, I will be grounded until high school—*

"Hold it." Sean stopped on the stairway landing, where a bare red bulb shed an eerie light. He held the map close to his face, then turned it over to view the back. "Wait a sec— Lottie wrote some kind of note here. It says that we have to post the ad in the..." He squinted at the paper. "The Ladies Cloakroom."

"What's a cloakroom?" Ronan asked, grinning. "Can we buy a Cloak of Invisibility there?"

"I wish," said Morgan, sliding past the boys to take the lead. As they trooped down the remaining stairs, she thought hard. "I think I read in an old-fashioned story that..." she stopped in an even dimmer hallway, barely illuminated by another red light. "A cloakroom is a restroom."

Directly in front of them was a door marked "Ladies," with bright yellow "Caution" tape crisscrossed over it, like the broken elevator on the TV show *The Big Bang Theory.* There was a small sign on the door behind the tape. *Closed for Repairs.*

This goofball hunt was going from bad to worse. "Well, Ronan, you wanted spooky. I think you got it." And now she had to give the boys the bad news. She nodded at the Ladies door. "We've got to get the flyer posted in there."

"No way," said Sean. "No girls' bathrooms. And boys aren't supposed to go in them anyway."

"I'm not going into the girl's bathroom either!" declared Ronan. "Yuk!"

"We can't go in even if we wanted to," Sean objected. "The tape means we're supposed to stay out. We could get into *big* trouble if we pulled the tape down."

We passed big trouble a long time ago, Morgan thought. And by now, she just wanted to get this dorky hunt over with. "Look guys, either we go in and finish the job, or just forget it."

12

Danger Downstairs

Ronan crossed his arms, a stubborn look on his face. "No. Girls. Bathrooms."

"But we've got to do the job right!" Sean eyed the hallway, a comically desperate look on his face. Then his gaze returned to Morgan's. "Okay, here's the solution. You do it."

"Do what?"

"Go into the bathroom by yourself and post the flyer."

"You *are* the girl here," Ronan pointed out.

I don't want to go in alone! Morgan wanted to say. But she didn't want her cousins to think she was a sissy, when Sean and Ronan had been brave and up for every twist and turn of this hunt...Except a girls' bathroom. And if she wanted to be all grown up, she couldn't wimp out on something as simple as going into some icky old basement room... "What if there's a good reason the caution tape is up? Like, there's no floor or something!"

"Morgan's got a good point," said Ronan. "If there's no

light in there, she won't be able to see where to post the paper."

"We can't decide until we get the door open," Sean said calmly and pulled out his Nerfball. "Maybe we can get some extra glow off my ball."

Trepidation running through her, Morgan helped the boys pull the Caution tape down and toss it aside. She carefully turned the doorknob. The door wouldn't move. *Jeez—another old sticking door!* Pushing harder, Morgan finally eased the door open a crack, and a loud *creak* echoed through the hallway. "Oh!" Morgan froze. "They could probably hear that upstairs!"

"Of course they can't," Sean said. "It's so loud up there no one can hear anything."

"Oh, great," murmured Morgan. She felt a strong, cold draft of air pouring out of the bathroom, like she was in front of an air conditioner turned to high. And it stunk! "Can you smell that?"

Ronan sniffed. "It smells fishy and seaweedy. Kinda like the river."

"Could be worse," said Sean.

"Yeah, it could smell like something died in there." Ronan turned on his flashlight.

"Oh, you've made me feel *lots* better," Morgan said, opening the door wider. She stuck her hand inside, feeling around for a light switch. Nothing. "Guys, without more light, I can't—"

"Come on, you can do it," encouraged Ronan. He shone the small beam of light inside, revealing just an average dingy public restroom with a high ceiling. There were three stalls and a big air vent grill with wide slits above a dusty sink.

Morgan scanned the room. The walls were stained, the mirror mottled, and the linoleum floor was dirty, but at least there *was* a floor. Still, she hesitated. "Guys, get the tape ready, please. I want to make this fast."

Setting the Nerf ball into the sink, Sean fumbled in his backpack, then passed her a flyer and a length of tape. Holding the flyer with shaking hands, Morgan tried to stretch the tape across the top edge, but the tape promptly stuck itself to the back of the flyer. "I goofed—need more tape."

Sean patiently unwound more tape and handed it to her. Morgan took a cautious step inside the bathroom, then another, ready to attach the flyer to the mirror. Another strong draft of air hit the room. Morgan shivered, then just as quickly, she felt a powerful rush of air flow out of the bathroom. The paper flew out of her hand and upward. In the dim light, Morgan could just make out the flyer—it had been sucked against the vent above her head! "Oh, no!"

"What—what?" the boys said in unison.

"I let go of the flyer and now I can't reach it! I need another one, quick—"

"We don't have any more flyers," said Sean, his voice worried. "Lottie only gave us enough to—"

"Never mind that!" Morgan boosted herself onto the sink, then heard an ominous, crunching noise... Was the sink starting to detach from the wall? She promptly jumped down. "Guys, you've got to get in here and help me—"

"We told you. No. Girls. Bathrooms," said Sean.

Morgan turned around to open the door wide, facing her cousins with her hands on her hips. "Get over it, guys! I need you in here, or our Scavenger Hunt will be a failure!"

The boys looked at each other with resigned expressions. "O-*kay.*" Ronan sighed theatrically and stepped into the bathroom.

Sean followed, peering around like the Girls' Bathroom Police were lurking nearby, waiting to arrest him. "What do we do now?"

"You two get over here and prop up the sink, while I climb up."

The boys supported the sink on either side as Morgan scrambled up. Reaching for the flyer against the grill, she felt another cold draft rush into the room. Then the air rushed out again like before. But this time, the draft pulled the flyer right through a slit in the vent grill!

Morgan groaned. "Did you see what happened? Our flyer is gone! I say we bag this whole thing and get out of here!"

"Aw, come on," Ronan coaxed, holding his side of the sink up. "We're almost done."

"We've come this far," said Sean. "I say we pull the grill from the wall and get our flyer."

Standing on the sink, Morgan balanced herself. "And how are we supposed to do that?" She stuck her fingers through the grill and tried to wiggle it. Surprisingly, the grill shifted. "Wait," she said, "it's really loose. Maybe we can get this thing off after all."

"Jump down," Sean ordered, still supporting the sink. "Lemme see if I can do it." As Morgan clambered down, he said, "Do you still have that funny-looking key from the arcade?"

"Well, yeah," said Morgan, pulling it from her jeans pocket and handing it over.

"Here, take a turn holding the sink," said Sean. Morgan positioned herself on his side of the sink, then he climbed up. Sliding the skeleton key into a small space between the wall and the vent, he worked the key back and forth for a few seconds. He pulled on the grill gently, and it came free!

Balancing on the sink, Sean dropped the grill carefully to the floor. "How about that?" He passed the key back to Morgan.

"But do you see the flyer?" asked Morgan.

Sean reached in, then produced the piece of paper. "Got it." He set it down on the edge of the vent opening, glancing into the dark space. "I swear there's...well, I think there's something back here. Ronan, hand up your flashlight."

Holding his side of the sink with one arm, Ronan complied. Sean shone the tiny light into the vent. "I was right!"

"Will you just get the flyer, please?" Morgan could not *wait* to get out of here.

"Whoa! I think there's a tunnel back here—"

"Guys, can we just do the job?" Morgan couldn't let them get sidetracked—not when they were this close to being done!

"There's a gravelly floor," said Sean. "Like a cave. And the ceiling is taller than me." He dropped the flashlight into Ronan's outstretched hand. "Let's check it out!"

Just then, still another blast of cold, fishy air blew into the bathroom, and the flyer sailed back out of the vent, swirling around the room above their heads.

"You're not getting away this time!" cried a voice. Morgan turned horrified eyes toward the door to see the stalker teen standing there. The dim red light in the hallway gave the boy's angry face a macabre glow. "Tell me NOW!" he roared, snatching the paper as it floated downward. "How do you know Letitia?"

"Morgan—up on the sink! Into the tunnel!" yelled Sean.

"I can't!" The sink would break for sure with her weight added to Sean's. "And Mom said we've got to stick together!"

13

Into the Dark

His face vicious, the boy took a menacing step inside the bathroom. Sean jumped off the sink toward the door, lunging to hit the teen on the head. He missed, only pulling the boy's kerchief off, revealing thick curly hair. As his head snapped back, Ronan let go of the sink and grabbed the boy's sunglasses and flung them aside. There was a *crack*, then Ronan shone his flashlight straight into their intruder's eyes.

"Don't! The light hurts!" Dropping the flyer, the boy reeled backwards, holding up his hands to block the beam of light. Morgan saw that one of his eyes looked funny. "It burns my eyes!" He turned away, collapsing against the wall.

"INTO THE TUNNEL, NOW," screamed Sean. "It's our only chance of escape!"

Morgan scrambled onto the sink then boosted herself into the vent space. *I can't think about spiders and worms now!* She crawled into the tunnel.

"Now me," cried Ronan, climbing up. In an instant, he was inside the wall next to Morgan.

Kneeling near the vent hidey-hole, she watched as Sean plucked his Nerfball from the sink and jumped onto it, the boy still crouched on the floor. She heard a crunching sound as Sean braced himself on the edge of the opening. The sink gave way, a crash echoing through the bathroom. Legs dangling, Sean eased into the vent space alongside Morgan and Ronan, cradling his ball.

"We're safe," Ronan crowed. "He can't climb up way up here without the sink!"

"Safe to go where?" Morgan asked, hugging herself. The teen was slowly staggering to his feet. Maybe he'd give up and let them alone, now that they were out of reach...

"Maybe there's a way out of here, leading to the river!" said Sean. "That seaweedy smell, remember?"

"I just want to get out of this bathroom," said Ronan, pointing his flashlight into the tunnel. The small light traveled only a few feet. He clicked it back off.

"And go where?" Morgan asked. At least *one* of her cousins was finally sick of this scavenger hunt.

"The only way out," said Sean, pointing into blackness.

"I wouldn't take that way if I were you," a voice said suddenly, and the top of a curly head showed in the open vent space. As the teen's face came into view, it was contorted with rage, his dark glasses looking like the eyes of a giant insect, one lens badly cracked. "Don't think you'll ever get away!"

Morgan scuttled backwards. *How had he gotten up here?* "What do we do?" The boy held up his hands like claws, then he fumbled around the vent. "We're trapped!"

"Just follow the glow!" said Sean, drawing back his arm to toss his Nerf ball into the blackness of the tunnel. The ball sailed through the air, then hit the floor and started rolling. "And RUN!"

Without thinking, Morgan bounced to her feet and took off, keeping her eyes on the dim green ball of light moving ahead, the boys tearing through the tunnel right behind her.

Running into the blackness was the scariest thing she'd ever done her entire *life*. All she could hear was hers and the boys' labored breathing, and the crunch of their footsteps on the gravel beneath their feet. Following the faint green glow, she was sure that any minute her head could crash into an unseen obstacle on the ceiling of the tunnel—or they would all fall into a deep chasm, never to be seen again.

Then Morgan sensed something else—an instinct—and suddenly she knew the teen was in the tunnel behind them in hot pursuit. "Keep running, guys!" she gasped. She sprinted on, not knowing how much longer her lungs would hold out.

Morgan felt like she and the boys had been running forever. Sure that her legs would give out any second, she forced herself to keep going no matter what. Keep moving, faster, faster...

Then it happened. All at once, the Nerf ball rolled to a stop, and the seaweedy odor was almost overpowering. She heard the sound of water lapping. The river! "Stop!" she screamed. Morgan and her cousins skidded on the gravel, almost colliding into a wall of rubble.

The boys huddling beside her, Morgan pressed her back against the rocky wall, feeling the teen stalker coming closer. "He'll be here soon," she whispered, knowing their pursuer was swiftly closing the gap between them. *I'm so sorry, guys.* She was too terrified to say it out loud. Or even cry.

Because this time, they really *were* completely and totally trapped.

Morgan felt like she was going to throw up. *The creepy teen will get us—and it's all my fault.* "Be brave," she managed to croak to her cousins, and braced herself as the teen approached.

"You'll answer my questions now!" he bellowed from the darkness. "WHAT DO YOU KNOW ABOUT LETITIA?"

Suddenly, Sean stepped in front of her protectively. Ronan slid next to his brother, fumbling for his flashlight. He turned it on, shining the light toward the teen.

The boy stumbled into view, shielding his eyes. His face bitter, he stopped a short distance away, throwing a crumbled up piece of paper at them. "How can you do this?"

Morgan could feel her cousins' bodies trembling, even worse than hers. But protecting her, they'd shown a new grownup kind of courage... "This what?" Her voice shook so badly she hardly recognized it.

"This horrible joke!" cried the boy.

"What joke?" Ronan pointed his flashlight at the teen's face. His arcade gizmo was their only defense.

The teen jerked his head to avoid the light, clenching his fists. "Your advertisement—it's a terrible, cruel hoax!" he yelled. How could you do something so spiteful? So...so vile?"

"What are you talking about?" Sean asked. "It's not a joke. Lottie told us to—"

"You're lying! She can't have told you anything—not now, not ever!"

"Why not?" Morgan gripped the rock behind her so hard her fingers stung.

The teen's mouth twisted, and Morgan saw something new in his face. Grief. "Because she's dead!"

14

The Discovery

*D*ead? Lottie was *dead*?

When their stalker didn't make a move to hurt them, Morgan drew a deep breath. *I may not puke after all.* "Now you're the one who's lying." She tapped Sean on the shoulder. As he shifted, she squeezed between her cousins, so all three of them faced the boy squarely. "We just saw Lottie today."

"Yeah," said Ronan. "We talked to her."

"And she talked to us," Morgan said. "A *lot.*"

The boy's expression hardened. "Where did you see this girl? What did she look like?"

"Upstairs, at the Lahti mansion," Ronan said promptly.

"She was about fourteen," said Morgan. "With long blond hair. And a lacy dress."

"And pretty," Sean added, and even in the near-darkness, Morgan could swear she saw him blush. "Though her dress was awfully dirty."

The boy's face changed.

"She was really bossy, too," said Ronan.

She's the one who made those ads," said Morgan, "and practically *forced* us to put them up around town."

The teen crumpled to the ground. "That can't be." He buried his face in his hands.

Ronan shone his flashlight around the teen. Even in the dim light, Morgan could see that his uncovered hair was vivid...red. Unbelievably, they'd found—

"Wait—you're...Billy!" Ronan exclaimed. "The guy in the flyer! Lottie wants to talk to you!"

The boy looked up. "I'm B-Billy S-S-mith," he stammered. He looked ready to cry. "But Lottie, she c-couldn't...she *can't* have been behind this..."

"Lottie *was*," said Morgan. She was still frightened, but this boy—Billy—well, he no longer seemed like a threat. Not with the way he crouched on the ground, limp as a wilted flower. "She's been looking for you."

Billy shook his head in disbelief. "I...I...that's not possible."

"Why not?" said Sean.

"In the winter," said Billy, "she...she got really sick. Lung fever." His mouth trembled. "And she died from it."

Morgan's mind swirled. She'd experienced mysteries before, things that made no sense. Like when that

Halloween curse had been put on her. And when she'd lost her memory that Christmas Eve in her grandparents' woods, only sensing...dreaming of magical creatures deep in the forest. But *this*...

So...Lottie wasn't an actress, doing a publicity stunt? Or playing a really mean trick on them? Billy *couldn't* be faking such grief and confusion. "Does this mean that Lottie is a..." Morgan's voice trailed away.

"A ghost," Sean finished.

"A ghost," Ronan said consideringly. "Wow—we talked to a *ghost.*" He looked more closely at Billy. "By the way, I'm Ronan, that's Sean, and our cousin Morgan," he said with his usual knack for introductions. "What are you going to do to us?"

"Do to you?" Billy sounded baffled.

"Yeah. We want to know if you're going to hurt us."

"I'm not going to do anything to you," Billy said. The sorrow in his face convinced Morgan there was no way he was lying. "I just had to make you tell me about Letitia. That's all."

"Come *on!*" Morgan felt sorry for him, but after everything he'd put them through... "You've been acting pretty crazy and dangerous, threatening us and chasing us all through Astoria—you can't just shrug it off!"

"I'm sorry," Billy said feebly, trying to sit up straight.

As Morgan kept gazing at the defeated-looking boy, something occurred to her. *What would you have done in*

Billy's place, if your best friend Claire had died? And suddenly you find a bunch of kids are running around posting a flyer with your dead friend's face on it? She thought hard.

"Maybe you're the one who needs to tell us about Lottie," she said. "How you knew her...and how she..." Morgan swallowed. "How she died."

"Will you get that light out of my face first?" Billy asked. As Ronan aimed his flashlight sideways, Billy took off his sunglasses and swiped at his eyes. Morgan saw again that his left eye looked damaged. Could he even see out of it?

"It's a long story," Billy said finally, putting his glasses back on. "I don't know where to start—"

"We don't have a lot of time," Morgan told him. She pulled out her phone to check the clock. It was way past five! And it would take forever to go back to that super-icky Freedom Theatre bathroom through the tunnel, and through the crowds upstairs. "Do you know a shortcut to the Lahti place? Lottie—or her, um, ghost, expects us before six o'clock."

"And there's the contest too!" Sean put in. He picked up the Nerf ball from the ground. "We've got to hurry—"

"Shhh." Billy cocked his head. "Hear that?"

Morgan heard the sound of water again, louder than before. "The river?"

"Yes, we're at the river's edge, and the tide is in," said Billy. "We've got to stay here for at least a quarter hour, before the tide goes out enough so you can get to the other tunnel."

"The other tunnel!" Ronan eyes gleamed. "I've got to hear about that!"

Jumpy with nerves and their approaching deadline, Morgan made herself sit down on the rough gravel. Ronan did too, and after another watchful look at Billy, Sean sat next to his brother. Morgan passed him the phone so he could see the time. Sean nodded and returned it. "Tell us first," he said. "About you and Lottie."

15

Lottie's Ghost

Billy didn't say anything for a moment. "I don't know if Letitia would want me to say anything—"

"You owe us the truth," Morgan said, "after scaring us to *death*." Oops. Wrong word.

Billy nodded. "Letitia was the only daughter of the most powerful man in Astoria," he began. "They lived in the grandest house in town. Letitia wanted an adventurous life, but her ma..." he shook his head. "Her ma wanted her to be a proper lady."

"We already know that," Morgan said impatiently. "Tell us something we don't!"

"Well," said Billy, "she would often break her ma's rules, and get sent up to her room for punishment."

"Would her room be the Tower Room?" asked Sean.

"Actually, yes," said Billy. "What her ma and pa didn't know was that every once in a while she'd sneak down the secret staircase and into the garden shed, to get to the smuggler's tunnel."

"The smuggler's tunnel," Ronan repeated, his eyes dancing with excitement. "Is this it?"

"Well," said Billy, "This is one of them. The other tunnel goes from under the Lahti's to the river—"

"Let's stick to Lottie," Morgan insisted. "Why did she sneak away from her house?"

"Her ma was making her go to some kind of school for young ladies in Portland, and Letitia was *furious* about it." A reminiscent smile crossed Billy's face. "She was too stubborn to let her ma make her do anything. And she had gumption—she wouldn't take bad fortune or punishment or anything else lying down."

Cranky gumption, thought Morgan. "And then?"

His smile faded. "The day before they were going to send her away, she ran deeper into the tunnel—almost to the end, near the high tide mark. She was going to stay overnight there, and teach her ma a lesson. But that night..." his face went bleak. "There was a terrible earthquake. The riverfront all but collapsed."

"Oh, no..." Morgan was afraid to hear any more. "Lottie didn't get...buried in the tunnel?"

"Worse," said Billy. His mouth tightened, as if he was trying not to sob.

Morgan pressed her hand to her throat. *What's worse than being buried alive? Poor Lottie...*

"Part of the tunnel fell in," Billy said finally, "and trapped Letitia at the water's edge. The tide came in even higher that night, but she had no way of getting out."

"She...drowned?" asked Sean, a worried look on his face.

Billy shook his head. "Almost," he said. "She got soaking wet, and there she was, caught in the tunnel in the dead of winter."

Morgan was more confused than ever. "How do you know all this? Or that she died at all?"

Billy stiffened. "I know because I...a fellow I know happened to be in the tunnels the next day, and he told me all about—"

"A smuggler?" said Ronan. He stuck his flashlight in his mouth, then managed to pull his book and pen from his backpack to jot something down. "Did he live down there?"

"He...uh, did," said Billy, sort of like he didn't want to say it. "That's why he was down there at all, and—"

"Never mind the smuggling!" said Morgan. "We're almost out of time. What happened then?"

"This...fellow heard Letitia crying for help, and he managed to dig an opening in the rubble, enough to get her out. By that time, she was terribly ill. He carried her through the tunnel to the Lahti's garden shed."

"Of course," said Ronan. "No wonder the shed smells like the river." He wrote something else.

"The fellow said that Letitia was hardly breathing by then," said Billy, his voice strained. "He got her out of the shed and to the kitchen door, then set her on the step and banged on the door with all his might. He ran back to the shed before anyone could see him."

"Why did he run away?" asked Sean. "Wouldn't he want to get credit for saving Lottie?"

"But that's just it—he didn't save her!" said Billy, his torment clear. "Her parents found her and got her inside. Mr. Lahti, her pa, was in his new motorcar in a second, to get the doctor..."

Motorcar? Morgan leaned forward, almost forgetting their time crunch. "Wasn't the doctor able to do anything?"

Billy shook his head, tears leaking from his damaged eye. "The...fellow was still watching when the doctor came. He couldn't leave without knowing what had happened to Letitia. A while later, the doctor was saying goodbye to her pa in the doorway. He was clasping Mr. Lahti on the arm, while her pa bowed his head and cried like a baby."

Morgan's heart squeezed. "I guess...that's pretty good evidence that she didn't make it." As Billy's jaw worked, she wondered if he would burst into tears right in front of them. "I'm really sorry." She reached out to touch Billy in sympathy.

Before she could, Billy lurched to his feet. "The earthquake cave-ins changed the tunnels quite a bit, but I think the tide's out far enough for you to get out." He headed toward the sound of lapping water.

Morgan scrambled to her feet. *There's more to this*

106

story.... Before she could say anything, Ronan was sliding his book into his pack, and Sean was cramming the Nerf ball into his own to follow Billy. Morgan brought up the rear. *How strange, to be trusting the boy we'd thought was our enemy, to get us out of here...*

As they walked, Ronan's flashlight illuminating their way, the fishy, seaweedy smell got stronger. Moments later, Morgan slipped a little on the rocks beneath her feet. Wet rocks. "We've reached the river, haven't we?"

"You'll get your shoes wet," Billy answered up ahead.

Sean and Ronan were stepping into the river shallows as Morgan detected a faint light. She walked into the water behind her cousins, felt the chilly water seep into her sneakers to her ankles. What would it have been like for Lottie, to feel the cold water rise to your legs, your waist, and up to your neck? What would it be like, to know the water would keep rising, that you'd drown any moment... She stopped cold. "Wait—Billy!" she called.

He stopped, turning to face her.

"Come on," said Sean, but he and Ronan stopped too. "I'll bet it's way past five."

"This is important," said Morgan. "Billy, if Lottie is a...a ghost, how come she could talk to us? Or make her ads? She had it planned perfectly too, how we could get them around town. How could she do all that?"

Billy smiled sadly. "I think Lottie doesn't know she's dead. And if she does, she refuses to admit it."

16

A Boy Like Me

As Billy and her cousins began moving slowly, Morgan's feet grew numb in the cold water. She'd heard ghosts haunt places or people because they have unfinished business—or can't let go of their life here on earth... Still thinking, Morgan splashed out of the water, rock and piles of rubble on either side of her, forming a little cavern. *Lottie was probably trapped right around here.* "Wait, you guys," she called. "I need a minute."

Patting her hoodie pocket, she felt a couple of lumps. Her candle and Billy's box of matches—they hadn't fallen out! She drew them out struck a half-dozen matches against the rough side of the box, but they were all duds. "Just one more," she muttered. Morgan tried another match—and it flared into light! She dipped the lit match to the wick of her candle, the flame small but steady in the darkness. "I'm sorry about what happened to you, Lottie," she whispered. What else could you say to a spirit?

"It must have been horrible—but I think you were really brave."

She was also sorry she'd thought Lottie deserved a dunking. Morgan wanted to leave her candle there, but she knew it would end up in the river, and she didn't want a sea bird or something to eat it by accident. "Well," she said, "um, take care."

Blowing out the candle, she leaned toward the river to dip the hot wick into the water and stuck it back in her pocket. As she hurried to catch up, Morgan couldn't stop thinking of Lottie. Sure, she'd been bossy and superior, but anyone who'd spent their last minutes on earth in a dark, dank place was entitled to act however she liked.

A bright light appeared above the pathway ahead. As she and the boys drew closer, she could see it was a square of clear plastic. The Smuggler's Café was right above them—and they must have fixed the floor!

Billy stopped in the square of light, shading his eyes with his hand, then he gazed around with a perplexed expression.

"Do you know this place?" Morgan asked.

"I could swear this was where..." his voice trailed away.

"Where what?" Sean asked.

"Where I got—" Billy set his jaw. "It doesn't matter. The quake and aftershocks have changed everything down here."

"We're right here at the Café!" Ronan broke in, pointing

to the panel above them. "The contest entry is due soon."

"Can we get up to this building from here?" Morgan asked. "Sean and Ronan have a quick errand to do."

Billy shook his head, and began walking again. "You'll have to go to the end of this next tunnel, to the shed." He rounded a curve. Pointing into another dark opening, he disappeared into the blackness. "Then backtrack above ground," he said, his voice floating from the hole. Ronan pointed his flashlight into the opening, and he, Sean and Morgan followed Billy.

As they walked, Ronan peppered Billy with questions. "So how come you know so much about these tunnels?"

"I worked on my pa's schooner. We used the tunnels to bring...uh, things from the ship into town this way."

"What kinds of things?" asked Ronan.

"The kind we really weren't...supposed to," Billy told him.

"I thought so!" Ronan said triumphantly. "You *are* a smuggler, and your dad is too!"

Morgan stumbled on the rough ground. "I thought you said your dad was dead."

"He is," Billy said, his voice shaking a little. "Just before I met Letitia, Pa got caught with...well, never mind what he did, but he got put in the new county jail."

She kept her eyes on Ronan's beam of light. *That's the second time Billy's mentioned a new jail. I wonder where it is...*

110

"The last time I went to see him," Billy was saying, "he'd come down with the influenza."

"What's that?" asked Sean.

"A fancy name for flu," said Morgan.

"He was in a bad way," said Billy, "but he came to enough to tell me I'd have to make my own way. Before he passed on, he made me promise to go to school. That's where I met Letitia. She was the only good thing about that place, though."

"You didn't like school?" Sean asked.

"I liked it fine, before a boy who was sweet on Letitia got a bunch of fellows to give me a thrashing. One of them threw a rock at me and hit me in the eye."

"It still looks kinda bad," Ronan observed.

"Could be worse, though," said Sean.

"Yeah," said Ronan. "You could look as bad as Sloth from *The Goonies* movie."

"Who's that?" said Billy. "And what's a gooney?"

"It's another long story," said Morgan.

"Anyway," said Billy, "I don't see so good out of my eye that got hit."

Why didn't anyone take you to the doctor? Morgan wondered, but Billy's life sounded hard enough without her reminding him.

Ronan was quiet for a moment. "It seems like you don't see so well with the other eye either, Billy. How come light burns both your eyes?"

"I guess it's because I mostly stay in the tunnels—in the dark," Billy said. "Letitia is the one who gave me these dark glasses."

"I'm just sorry you got bullied," said Ronan. "That stinks. And...and I'm super-sorry I cracked your sunglasses."

"Doesn't matter," Billy said brusquely, but it seemed to Morgan that he was forcing himself to sound tough. "I quit going to school after I got the beating. Letitia found me in the tunnels a week later, to give me an eyepatch she'd sewn for me with her very own hands...but I lost it." Morgan heard the pain in his voice. Not like he'd had a crush on Lottie, but like he...*loved* her.

Some puzzle pieces began to slide into place...Lottie had wanted to find Billy, to give him a reward for *services rendered...* "Hey," Morgan said casually, "is there any chance you were in the tunnels when Lottie ran away from home?"

Billy stopped in his tracks. Then Morgan knew it for sure. "You were the one who rescued Lottie!"

"You're a hero!" said Sean.

"I never felt like a hero," said Billy, his shoulders sagging, then he shuffled forward again. "Just before I got Letitia back to the Lahti's house, she begged me, with the little breath she still had, to keep my finding her a secret." His voice was full of misery. "If her mother had found out she'd been meeting a boy in the tunnels—especially a boy like me—"

"What's wrong with you?" asked Ronan. "You're cool. Like a...a pirate!"

"But I'm poor. And I've got no family," said Billy. "Or proper schooling. If Mrs. Lahti knew about me, she would have sent Letitia away a lot further than Portland. You won't tell anyone, will you?"

"Of course not," said Morgan.

"I won't tell either," Ronan promised.

"Back to your school," said Sean. "How could you quit and not have the principal and teachers make you go back?"

"No one can force you to go to school." Billy sounded surprised. "And like I told you, I had to find a job. And I wanted to have adventures!"

Like Lottie. Morgan pulled out her phone to check the time, feeling even more anxious. *If we're late, will Lottie, or her ghost, haunt us...like, forever?*

"I had a dangerous close call myself," said Billy. "The day after Letitia died, I was back down in the tunnels, and there was some aftershocks. I'd gone there to—" he broke off, shrugging.

"To do what?" Morgan asked.

"Well, to leave some flowers, where Letitia had been trapped."

Lottie would have liked that, thought Morgan.

"But the tunnel I was in had weakened. There was another cave-in, and I got banged on the head. In fact, I blacked out for a while, I think." Billy sounded really perplexed. "But I managed to dig myself out. Right now I'm waiting for another likely ship to come into port, and see if I can find work as a deckhand."

"Wow," said Ronan. "You're *super* cool. You should have your own YouTube channel."

"What's a you tube?" asked Billy.

Something clicked in Morgan's brain. Everything about this hunt that hadn't made sense suddenly...did. *Billy used the old-fashioned word "motorcar"... As young as he is, he doesn't have to go to school...Even though his parents are dead, he isn't in foster care...Billy doesn't know about YouTube...The Film Museum had once been the County Jail, brand-new in 1914 —*

"Wait a minute!" Phone in hand, she stumbled toward the boys, to catch up. *And there had been a big earthquake about a hundred years ago...*

Billy and her cousins turned to face her.

"Morgan, make it fast," said Sean. "We've got to hurry!"

"We're almost to the shed," said Billy.

Morgan saw the empty space ahead was starting to look sort of grayish, instead of black.

"I need a sec," said Ronan. He passed Sean the flashlight, then started scribbling something else on a sheet of paper.

Morgan could barely make out Billy's face. "When did you say Lottie died?"

"It was winter," said Billy, his face sad again. "I can still see her white face, her skin like wax. She was struggling so, to breathe at all, but she wanted to tell me goodbye. Her last words to me were—"

"I mean, the year!" cried Morgan. "What year did she die?"

"Why, this year," said Billy. "Just months ago."

Morgan squeezed her phone in frustration. "Then tell me, what year are we in?"

"Everyone knows what year it is," Billy said. "It's 1915."

Morgan's phone hit the ground with a thud. Sean dropped the flashlight.

Ronan gasped. "You're a ghost too!"

"Like Lottie!" said Sean in a harsh whisper.

Morgan struggled to find her voice. "And just like Lottie," she managed, "you don't know you're dead either."

115

17

The Tunnel Ends

Two ghosts.

She, Morgan Carey, had spent the afternoon with *ghosts*. And discovered that these spirits only wanted was what they'd missed out on while they were alive.

As Morgan picked up her phone, they were all silent. "Why...why do you think I'm a ghost?" Billy finally asked, his voice tremulous.

Sean said kindly, "It's actually 2015."

Billy gasped. Morgan heard him swallow a sob. "I guess..." he sniffed. "That when the tunnel caved in on me, I didn't just black out."

"Fraid not," said Ronan.

"You're taking finding out you're dead pretty well," Sean observed.

Billy swiped at his nose. "Life wasn't so good anyway."

Morgan, Billy and the boys moved through the rest of the tunnel in silence. "But Billy—" Morgan spoke up.

"Didn't you notice how...different the town was today? Above ground, I mean."

"Not really," said Billy in a faraway voice. "My eyesight is actually pretty bad."

"But Billy," Morgan said, "I get that Astoria looks sort of like it did one hundred years ago, but everything else—the cars, the stores, the way people dress—the town would have seemed like another world." She suddenly remembered all the people in oddball costumes today.

"It's true, the town looked pretty topsy-turvy," replied Billy. "I thought there was some kind of exposition going on. My ma had been to the Chicago World's Fair when she was young, and told me all about the new-fangled inventions on display. And that people had come from all over the world to gawk at all sorts of buildings and machines no one could have ever even imagined before. I thought Astoria was having something like that."

From what Morgan knew, a world's fair in the olden days would have been as awe-inspiring as Disney World's Epcot Center, not a small-town festival about a cult movie like *The Goonies*. Still, she kept her mouth shut as Billy took the lead toward the grayness ahead. "If only I could..." his voice trailed away. "Forget it," he said, his voice rough. "Ghosts don't get to have dreams."

Morgan pondered Billy's situation as all four of them hiked up a slight incline in the tunnel, the grayness growing brighter. He'd been through so much. He deserved something better than, *Oh, I guess I'm dead.* No one had mourned him—he hadn't even had a *funeral* or anything.

The tunnel space narrowed. Morgan and the three boys had to drop to all fours to ascend the last few feet, until they reached a hole just above them, covered with canvas. "This has to be that other opening to the garden shed," said Morgan.

"So from the shed, you can get to the river *and* the secret staircase," Ronan said. He pushed on the heavy canvas, shifting it a tiny bit, lightening up their space. "This shed has more holes than...Swiss cheese!"

Ronan could find the humor in anything, Morgan thought fondly. She felt a strange reluctance to end their adventure. Especially when Billy said regretfully, "This is where I leave you."

"Do you have to?" asked Ronan.

"I've been...lonesome, but you three made my life...well, my afterlife better. I just wish..." He swallowed hard. "Forget it."

Morgan shivered. Would ghosts just keep haunting, until they found some kind of...peace? Maybe Billy could get something...well, *special* from their time together. "Before you go," Morgan said, "Would you mind telling us Lottie's last words to you?"

Billy's smile was bittersweet. "I knew she was a goner. But even though she was nearly unconscious, she whispered, 'I know I'll see you again. Even if it's only once in a blue moon.'"

Morgan's eyes widened.

"Wait just one minute!" said Sean, and he and Ronan said in unison, "Right now, there *is* a blue moon!"

"Maybe you're supposed to see Lottie today!" Morgan said, excitement spiraling through her. She reached up and shoved aside the canvas, revealing a triangle-shaped opening. Daylight filled the tight space around them.

Billy yanked up one hand to shield his eyes. "Do you...do you think she would want to see me?"

Even with his eyes covered, Morgan could see the hope in his face. "After all the trouble she went to, to track you down? Of course! And maybe this chance for you to see Lottie is why all this happened!"

"All this?" asked Billy.

"Yes! Mom and me staying at The Lahti House, Lottie haunting the place, the Café contest, last night's earthquake—everything! It was meant to be!"

"And don't forget *The Goonies'* Anniversary Celebration," Ronan put in.

Billy's brow wrinkled, but Morgan couldn't explain the Anniversary now. He'd probably never even seen *any* movie, ever. "Everyone up, out of the tunnel! Then I'm taking Billy to the staircase."

Morgan poked her head above ground, finding herself in one corner of the shed, and climbed through the opening.

As she got to her feet on the canvas floor, her cousins eased their way through the hole.

Billy stayed crouched just below the opening, as if he didn't know what to do next. "Do you really believe that's possible?" His voice quavered. "Seeing Letitia?"

"After hanging out with two ghosts, I think anything is," said Morgan. "Let's go!"

"Me and Sean won't go with you—we'll head for the kitchen instead," said Ronan.

"Yeah, I'm hungry," said Sean. "I need a snack."

"We don't have time to eat," said Ronan. "We need to finish the contest entry—we barely have fifteen minutes!"

"Guys, wait a minute," said Morgan. "We can't *ever* let our moms know what we were up to today. Promise not to tell? No one would believe us anyway."

"I promise," Sean said solemnly.

"Pinky swear," said Ronan, linking his pinky finger with Morgan's. Sean reached out and curved his finger around theirs.

They wiggled their pinkies then let go. "Now we've got to finish our entry," said Sean.

"Lottie might have locked up the house," said Morgan, digging into her jeans' pocket. She pulled out two keys. Two *skeleton* keys. One from the B&B, the other from the arcade. "Oh." She stared hard at them. "I can't remember which is which."

"Let me see," said Sean. He matched up the two keys,

pressing them together so he could study their outlines. "They look...identical."

"We'll take both," said Ronan.

"Okay," said Morgan. "After all the mystical, amazing things that happened today, I wouldn't be surprised if both keys will open the lock."

The boys had to strain once again to open the shed door, but finally it creaked on its hinges, and they were off to the house. "The door was stuck when I was in here earlier, watching the house," said Billy, adjusting his glasses. "When I heard you three coming from the hidden staircase, I had to climb out of the window as fast as I could."

So ghosts, when they were doing their haunting, still had to get around just like people, Morgan reflected. But all she said was, "Okay, Billy—let's get you upstairs."

As Morgan stepped across the shed to the other opening, her eyes caught a flash of red on the window frame. But she had Billy's destiny to take care of. She pulled aside the board that led into the wooden passage, letting Billy scuttle from the floor hole to behind the wall. "Wait a sec—I can't see in the dark like you can." Morgan paused to pull out the candle and matches again. After three tries this time, she got a match to work and lit her candle.

Shielding the small flame with her hand, she followed Billy through the passage to the bottom of the dusty staircase. He moved quickly up the stairs but didn't appear to be winded at all. Just like after he'd climbed the Astoria Column. The advantage of being a ghost, thought Morgan. You don't need oxygen.

Billy stopped on the staircase landing. "I'll wait here while you go up and fetch Letitia. I don't want her to get into trouble, for having me in the house."

"But Billy, remember it's one hundred years later— Lottie's parents are long gone!" Morgan said in exasperation. "She won't have any more rules."

Billy shook his head stubbornly. "We always met in the dark. I won't change things now."

Poor guy, Morgan thought. Maybe he didn't want Lottie to see his damaged eye, since he'd lost his eyepatch. *Eyepatch....* "If that's what you want," she said slowly.

Morgan left Billy on the landing, and scooted up the second flight of stairs. Still holding her candle, she crawled through the short passage awkwardly to the cubbyhole. When she reached the trap door, she squeezed her eyes shut for a second. *Lottie, please still be haunting the Tower Room!* Drawing a breath, she tapped on the top of the cubby.

"Lottie," she said softly. "We finished the job. I've got the proof you wanted—and something else."

18

Spirits on the Stairs

Silence.

Morgan didn't know what to do next. Has Lottie already returned to the other world? Where ghosts live?

Then she heard a rattle. The square board above her shifted. Lottie, paler than ever, was kneeling at the edge of the trap door glaring down at Morgan. "It's about time," she said sharply. "It's nearly six!"

"Well, hello to you too," said Morgan, climbing out of the cubby. She blew out her candle, too excited to let ol' Lotto—or maybe Lotto's cranky spirit—get to her.

Morgan wished she could spend more time around Lottie—this might be her last chance to get a good look at a real, live ghost. Or at least a real dead one. Instead, she went straight to the bed, emptying her pockets of all the tickets, tokens, and the Fort Astoria wood splinters from her jeans and hoodie. "See? We did it!" Morgan lined up the items on the lace bedspread. "Got the ad up in all the places

123

you wanted." Lottie didn't need to know they never had gotten around to posting the flyer in the Freedom Theatre girls' bathroom.

"Well, it would appear you completed the job," said Lottie, surveying the bed. She flounced to the window seat—the cushion was still lying askew on the floor—and opened the top, bracing the lid against the window ledge. She pulled out her velvet bag of coins, then turned. "Where are the boys? I always pay my debts properly."

"I'll give them their money," said Morgan, holding out her hand.

Lottie gave her a suspicious look. "Can I trust you?"

"For Pete's sakes, Sean and Ronan are my cousins! Of course I'll give them their pay."

Sighing theatrically, Lottie opened the bag, took out three silver dollars, and dropped them into Morgan's outstretched hand. "There you go. Now be off with you."

Morgan rolled her eyes. Lottie really *did* have a princess complex! "I don't think so, Your Highness—I think it's you who should be off."

Lottie looked down her white nose at Morgan. "I *beg* your pardon?"

Morgan grinned. "You'd better get down that trapdoor, to the secret staircase. And bring your bag of money."

Lottie froze. "And...and why would I need that?"

"To pay someone for *services rendered*, of course," said Morgan.

"You...you haven't found—"

"Yes," said Morgan.

Instantly, Lottie's face went soft. She smoothed her hair, shook out her skirts, then pinched her cheeks. "Thank you," she said, and for the first time, she wasn't snarky at all.

"No problem," said Morgan. Lottie's wackadoodle scavenger hunt had been the reason she and the boys had had their amazing adventure—well, after getting the stuffing scared out of them! "So what are you waiting for?"

Lottie said hesitantly, "Mama and Papa did forbid me to leave the house."

"Doesn't the staircase count as the house?" asked Morgan. "Besides, I think you disobeyed your parents before."

Lottie bit her lip. "I've been trying to be a better daughter. At least lately. And I don't want to disappoint them ever again."

But Billy will be heartbroken if he can't see you... Morgan gave her an encouraging smile. "For a really good cause, like you said before, it's okay to bend the rules a little."

"Perhaps just this once." Lottie seemed to go a shade paler as she climbed into the cubbyhole. Morgan watched her slide easily into the passage, then she opened the bedroom door and rushed out. It would have been too snoopy to eavesdrop on Lottie and Billy's reunion. Besides, she had one more task to do.

She raced downstairs to the kitchen, finding both boys bent over a piece of paper. Scribbling madly, Ronan didn't even look up. Sean was munching on an apple. "We've almost got the entry done," he said.

"Great," said Morgan, grasping the knob of the outside door.

"What's that word for when you're so sick you can't breathe?" asked Ronan. "Your...um, lungs are full of goopy junk so you're like..." Gasping, he bugged out his eyes and stuck out his tongue, making a rattling sound in his throat.

"Asthma?" asked Sean.

"Nah." Ronan put on his normal face. "It's worse. People used to die from it all the time."

"Pneumonia?" Morgan guessed.

"I think that's it," said Ronan. "How do you spell it?"

Morgan spelled out the word, then she said, "You're watching the clock, right?"

"I know, it's almost six," said Ronan, signing the paper with a flourish.

Sean signed it too, looking concerned. "How will we get our entry to the Café in time?"

"I dunno," said Morgan. "Trust?"

The boys looked at each other and shrugged. Morgan wrenched the kitchen door open. She tore to the garden shed and shoved the door open, searching the small space. There it was—a flash of red, nearly obscured by the mildewed curtains.

She pushed the curtains aside and carefully plucked the piece of soft red fabric off the nail head it had caught on. The cloth was a little tattered, but anyone could see what it was. A red silk eyepatch.

Morgan ran back to the kitchen, ignoring her cousins' bemused looks, and up to the Tower Room. She climbed into the open cubbyhole, which gave her enough light to creep halfway down the first flight of stairs. Lottie was talking.

"We must say goodbye now—the moon will be setting soon. At six o'clock."

So that's why we had to get the job done by six, thought Morgan.

"But we will be seeing one another again, won't we?" Billy asked.

"At the next blue moon," Lottie promised.

Morgan found them on the landing, holding hands, Lottie's velvet bag sitting on a step. She held out the eyepatch. "I wanted to make sure Billy didn't leave without this."

Billy released Lottie's hand and took the piece of silk reverently. With great care, he slid the fabric over his curly head and settled the patch over his left eye. "I feel good as new now. Thank you."

"Billy," said Morgan. "If you don't mind my asking, where will you go now? Since you won't be working on a ship or anything."

"Back to the tunnels, of course," he said. "To the water's edge."

"The river has always been where he feels most at home," said Lottie, taking Billy's hand again.

Morgan nodded. "Goodbye, Billy," she said. "It was great...um, meeting you." She backed away, so he and Lottie could say their farewells in private.

A car engine rumbled outside. Swiftly returning to the Tower Room, Morgan was climbing out of the trapdoor when she sensed someone behind her.

"I don't have all day," said Lottie. And somehow she...well, passed *through* Morgan to enter the bedroom.

Morgan replaced the floor panel, then faced Lottie. Did she realize she was a ghost yet? And that Billy was one too? But whether she did or not, she and Billy had been able to see each other. Which was what really mattered. "And what will you do next?"

"I wait until the next blue moon, to see Billy," said Lottie. She seemed faded, almost transparent as she held out her velvet drawstring bag. "Here, you may have this— Billy said he didn't need any money."

Ghosts generally don't, thought Morgan, accepting the bag. "The lady who lives here could use it," she said. Maybe some cash would help the B&B stay in business. "Actually, she's a relative of yours."

"Please see that she gets it," said Lottie, as queenly as ever.

Morgan heard the boys say downstairs, "We've got to *hurry!*" followed by footsteps on the staircase to the Tower Room floor. She watched as Lottie moved...well, more like *floated* to the still-open window seat. The girl fluffed out her skirts again and stepped daintily into the space under the seat. Grasping the cover, Lottie said "Good-bye," and just...*disappeared.*

Morgan gasped as the seat lid closed gently over the empty space. She could swear the room still hummed with something. *Energy.* She could feel a strange vibration coming off the window seat, circling around the bed—

The bedroom door burst open. "Morgan!" said her mom, smiling. "Your aunt's driving the boys over to the Smuggler's Hole Café so they can turn in their entry—and we had a wonderful afternoon! How about you guys?"

"We had a pretty good day too," said Morgan. She hoped her mom never, *ever* found out what they'd been up to! "But you know, I think I'd like to change rooms for tonight. Can we ask Valerie if we can move to Room Three?"

19

The Smuggler's Hole

"I can't wait 'til tonight!" Sean said the next morning, biting into a breakfast burrito.

Sipping a smoothie, Morgan shaded her eyes as the sun broke from a bank of clouds over the Pacific Ocean. She and her mom, the boys, Aunt Shannon and the baby were having breakfast at the Smuggler's Hole Café. Actually, they were sitting at a picnic table outside the restaurant, which was still getting fixed up after the quake the night before last. The owners had set up a food truck in the restaurant's parking lot and brought in a bunch of tables, now crowded with people. "I can't wait either!" Ronan squealed.

Morgan looked across the table at her cousin. "You mean for *The Goonies* Anniversary closing ceremonies?"

"Who cares about that!" said Ronan, slurping his glass of orange juice. "We want to know the winner of the 'Name the Skeleton' contest!" He looked at his mom.

"You're taking us to the Theatre for the big celebration, right?"

"It starts at six o'clock," said Sean. "But we want to show up way before that."

"We'll get you there in plenty of time," said Morgan's mom. She bounced Mary Rose on her lap one more time, and passed the baby to Aunt Shannon.

Morgan grinned and leaned against her mother. It wasn't so bad, being a kid. In fact, maybe she'd like stay one a little longer. After yesterday, when she'd thought they'd get attacked by a stranger, and that she'd be responsible for her cousins getting hurt, she had to admit that being a grown up wasn't as great as she'd thought.

Although it had been really cool to help Valerie last night. "I...um, my cousins and I found this under the window seat upstairs." Morgan handed the B&B owner the velvet bag of money.

The woman looked inside the bag, her eyes filling with tears. "This is amazing—maybe a windfall like this is a sign I should hang in here with my B&B." She'd smiled at Morgan. "And it's so mature of you to turn it in—a lot of people would have just kept the money."

Now, Morgan watched more people gather outside the restaurant doors. Ms. Pink Hair, the server they'd met the other night, was winding her way through the picnic tables, holding a pitcher of juice. The woman came toward them. "Refills, anyone?"

"I'd love a little more," said Aunt Shannon, settling Mary Rose in the crook of her arm. "Say, the Café is officially closed, right?" she asked the server.

"Right." The woman's pink streaks gleamed fluorescent in the sunshine.

"So what all these people are doing here?" Ronan piped up, pointing at the crowd. Just then, a big white van with a satellite dish on the roof and "TV 12" emblazoned on the side pulled into the parking lot.

The server's eyes sparkled. "The Café is making the news!" She filled Aunt Shannon's glass and topped off Ronan's. "We've got a big surprise inside—maybe all of you should get in line before the whole town shows up!" Tilting the pitcher over Sean's glass, she suddenly set it down. "Hey kids—I remember you from the other night."

"Yeah," said Sean. "We were checking out the skeleton—before it got stolen."

"You guys entered the contest, right?" said the server. "So I think you three get special treatment. I'll take you inside myself, to see the surprise, before the TV people take over the place."

"You can do that?" asked Sean.

The server laughed. "I'm Marin, one of the owners of the Café. I think I can get away with it."

Morgan and the boys leaped from their benches. "Mom, you coming?" Morgan asked.

"You guys go ahead," said her mom. "I'll stay here and stare at my beautiful little niece."

"Who's just about ready to fall asleep," said Aunt Shannon, shifting Mary Rose onto her shoulder. "We'll wait here for you."

Marin made a beeline for the Café entrance, Morgan, Ronan and Sean at her heels, and they threaded their way through the crowd. "Excuse me," said Morgan, trying to stay close to Marin.

"S'cuse me," Ronan said, nipping around a family with a double stroller.

"Do you think it's all right, taking cuts?" Sean whispered to Morgan.

"Just this once," said Morgan, smiling.

They slipped inside the entrance just behind Marin. The restaurant floor was covered with sawdust and tarps. As they approached the fireplace, Morgan could see the square hole was surrounded by four poles, yellow "caution" tape wound around them. "Go ahead, take a look," Marin said indulgently. "But stay off the Plexiglas—the glue is still setting up." She looked down at the panel, shaking her head. "I still can't figure out how it happened."

"What happened?" asked Ronan.

"Well, we got the floor fixed and the plastic panel installed yesterday *afternoon.*"

"So what's the surprise?" Sean wanted to know.

"What's really mysterious is that *this*," and Marin pointed to the hole, "turned up sometime last night. *After* the panel was glued down." She headed for the kitchen.

What in the world was she talking about? Morgan approached the hole slowly, one cousin on either side of her. Not knowing what she'd find, she stopped at the tape barrier, and squeezed her eyes shut.

"Morgan!" hissed Ronan. "You won't believe this!"

She opened her eyes and peered down. There, illuminated by sunshine above the gently lapping river, was a skeleton. With a red silk eye patch perched jauntily over its skull.

Morgan felt faint. "You don't think it's..." she lowered her voice. "Billy?"

Sean nodded. "I think he's back where he belongs."

20

"And the Winner of the Contest Is..."

On the Freedom Theatre's stage, the emcee of *The Goonies* Anniversary Celebration stood in bright yellow light and smoothed her flowered dress. Clearing her throat, she turned up the microphone. "And a great big thank you to another one of our sponsors, Astoria's Dratted Cat Bistro..." Morgan sighed, pulling out her phone to check the time.

Ronan, sitting next to Morgan's mom, wriggled in his seat. "I just wish they'd get to the contest announcement."

"Maybe they forgot about the contest," said Sean, looking worried.

"They wouldn't do that," Aunt Shannon soothed, but Morgan was beginning to wonder if someone had dropped the ball on the contest. She and her cousins had tried to be patient with the gazillion thank you's, the handshakes, and the "Congratulations for a great job!" announcements. Even when the Anniversary organizers brought up a couple of actors from *The Goonies* movie to take some bows, Morgan hardly cared, feeling as antsy as her cousins. "Will you get to the contest already?" she said under her breath.

As if the emcee had heard Morgan, she grinned widely at the audience. "And now, the moment many of you have been waiting for..."

The hum of voices in the theatre rose, and a couple of kids squealed.

"Shhh," hissed Sean, as if that would help. Ronan sat straighter in his seat.

"The 'Name the Skeleton' contest sponsored by Smuggler's Hole Café!" said the emcee. Beaming as two others joined her on stage, she introduced a bald guy from the Heritage Museum and Marin from the Café. She wore a shiny pink dress that matched her hair streaks. "Many of you know about the skeleton under the Café, right?" said the emcee.

There were a few scattered, "yeahs" and hoots from the audience.

"The contest was all about who could come up with the best name for the skeleton, and the best story for how it got there." The emcee's face became serious. "Sad to say, despite getting over eighty entries..."

"...The contest wasn't much of a contest," finished the bald man.

Sean's face fell. "The contest was cancelled?"

"Shhh, Sweetie," whispered Aunt Shannon. "Let's just listen."

"What we mean to say," said Marin, her sequined dress glittering under the stage lights, "was that all of us on the contest committee thought we'd be up all night, trying to make our decision."

The emcee broke out into another big smile but didn't say anything.

"However, out of all the entries," Marin went on, "one was so creative and imaginative, so full of interesting details, that we knew it was the clear winner from the moment we read it."

"Which we will do now," intoned the museum guy, and the audience buzzed like a giant beehive. He held up a hand. "Ahem!" As people quieted, he began to read.

"The skeleton's name is Billy Smith, short for William, and he was the son of a smuggler in the olden days."

Sean's eyes went round, then his face split into a grin. "Are you kidding me?" he whispered.

"Oh! Oh!" Ronan popped up from his seat, then sat down again.

The man continued, "Billy lived around a hundred years ago. He worked with his dad on their boat that chugged up and down the Columbia River. They smuggled stuff through underground tunnels leading from the riverfront into Astoria. Which is against the law, but back then a lot of people got away with breaking the law because there weren't that many police around.

"Billy thought he and his dad were doing okay because they didn't get caught. But then his dad got arrested and sent to jail. He got really sick there and died. Billy decided he'd better quit the smuggling business and go to school. Although he met a pretty girl there he liked a lot, before he could get much education he got beat up by some bullies, and his eye was damaged.

"Although the pretty girl made him a cool red eyepatch to cover up his bad eye, which made him look like a pirate, Billy swore off school. He decided to hunker down in the tunnels and wait for another smuggling job, even though it was against the law. He and the pretty girl met secretly down in the tunnels, but one day there was a giant earthquake and part of the tunnels caved in. She got trapped down there and caught pneumonia. Billy managed to rescue her, but she died anyway."

The audience sighed, "Ooohhhh." A baby wailed.

"Billy was so sad he didn't know what to do next. Except hang out in the tunnels where he'd been happy, first with his dad, then the pretty girl. But a day later, there were some bad aftershocks from the big quake. Billy was under the old Astoria Mercantile store when there was another tunnel cave-in. He got conked on the head and he was a goner too."

A kid started to cry.

"His skeleton was found under the building, and when

the Smuggler's Hole Café moved in they decided to let the skeleton stay there. But the other night, when a new earthquake blew up the floor of the Café, Billy wanted one more chance to be happy. His spirit went looking for the pretty girl and what do you know? Her spirit was looking for him too and somehow they found each other. We think the two ghosts will get together every time there's a blue moon."

"Whoa, there really *was* a blue moon this weekend," someone said in the row in front of Morgan.

"Then Billy returned to his old spot underneath the Café," said the Museum guy, "wearing his eyepatch this time. There he will wait until the next blue moon, when he'll see the girl—"

People in the audience began clapping. The emcee held up a hand, but the clapping went on even more enthusiastically.

The museum guy raised his voice, practically yelling to make himself heard. "Billy can't go back to smuggling, of course, since he's dead. But it'll be okay—because as long as he stays under the Café, people will never forget him."

And we'll never forget you either, Lottie, Morgan said to herself as the applause grew. Soon the old theatre seemed to shake, and some loud whistles nearly raised the roof! The clapping continued until the emcee on stage held up her hands. "Thank-you, thank-you..." She peered into the audience, squinting against the lights. "Sean and Ronan

Eldon, are you there? Can you come to the stage?"

Morgan watched proudly as her cousins stood up and scooted down the row, then walked onto the stage. They stood straight, grinning, as the applause thundered. A photographer appeared from the wings and snapped dozens of pictures. The emcee took the mic again. "Boys, anything you want to say?"

Ronan shook his head shyly. "That's a first," Aunt Shannon whispered to Morgan's mom.

Sean, up on stage, seemed to swallow hard. He raised his hand.

"Yes, Sean?" The emcee handed him the microphone.

"This," Sean said into the mic with a voice that shook, "is the best day of my life. Wait—" and he paused. "Actually, yesterday and today have been the best *two* days of my life." He handed the mic back to her.

"You can read a printed version of the story in tomorrow's *Astoria Journal*," she said. "Let's give Sean and Ronan another round of applause!"

The audience didn't need encouragement to clap some more. But finally, Sean and Ronan returned to their seats, their faces shining. Ronan was waving the Winner's Certificate. Morgan was so proud she could bust, and Aunt Shannon was wiping tears from her eyes.

"Congratulations, boys," said a lady on one side of them, standing up to leave.

"Thanks," Ronan said.

"Awesome story!" a kid said behind them. Sean and Ronan turned around to face him. "But how did you know about the red eyepatch?" the boy asked. "You had to turn in your contest entry yesterday, but the skeleton didn't show up until today."

"Um..." began Sean. He and Ronan looked at each other, then at Morgan.

"Just a lucky guess, I bet," said Morgan.

As the boy sidled from his seat and down the aisle, Sean leaned close to Morgan. "We never did put the coolest thing of all in our entry," he whispered.

"What's that?" asked Morgan.

"Well," said Sean, "that Billy *could* have been the real-life inspiration for that legend from *The Goonies*."

"You know, the pirate guy with one eye," Ronan put in. "But no one will ever know for sure."

Morgan grinned at her cousins. "*The Goonies* is just a movie," she said. "But Billy and Lottie gave us a *real* adventure—the best scavenger hunt ever!"

The End

Author's Note

Like many storytellers have done before, I have played with some facts in order to make my story fit together!

Earthquakes do occur in the northwest corner of Oregon where Astoria is located, but historically, the town of Astoria has had more of a problem with fires. In fact, a blaze engulfed the town in 1922, so badly that many streets collapsed, and people were dynamiting buildings to keep other structures from catching fire.

These days, the Astoria Column is a popular locale for both city visitors and local residents, and was included in my story's plot. However, during the weekend of the 30th Anniversary Celebration of *The Goonies* film, June 5th, 6th, and 7th, 2015, the timeframe of this story, the Column was closed to visitors for remodeling.

Finally, in *The Secret Astoria Scavenger Hunt*, part of the plot hinges on a natural phenomenon known as a blue moon. In the story, the blue moon occurs during the month of June, 2015. In actuality, a blue moon occurred the following month, in July 2015, with a full moon on July 2nd, and the second one occurring July 31st.

If I've gotten any details wrong, I welcome corrections from readers—as well as any and all facts and legends about Astoria!

— Susan Colleen Browne

Morgan Carey and The Mystery of the Christmas Fairies
a gentle fantasy "novelette" for middle grade readers!

In Book 2 of the Morgan Carey series, Seattle fifth-grader Morgan makes a holiday visit to her grandparents' house in the foothills of the Cascade mountains. While Morgan thinks her grandma and grandpa are great and everything, they live way out in the boonies, with no cable TV or even cell phones! Sure she'll be totally bored, Morgan discovers it gets worse: on Christmas Eve, she's stuck looking after her three young step-cousins who she hardly knows.

Babysitting the unruly little kids during a jaunt in the woods, Morgan and her cousins are lured into an entrancing, mysterious forest, where they encounter unexpected adventures...and even dangers. Morgan must draw upon all her strengths and ingenuity—and the talents of her little cousins—if they are escape this magical world, and find their way back home for Christmas.

This heartwarming, family-friendly tale is for kids, grandparents, and anyone who is young at heart!

145

Thank you from Susan Colleen Browne!

Thanks so much for your interest in *The Secret Astoria Scavenger Hunt*. If you enjoyed reading this book, I hope you'll consider posting a review online! In any event, I'm deeply grateful for your support, and would love to hear from you at www.susancolleenbrowne.com or www.littlefarminthefoothills.blogspot.com

Acknowledgments

Deepest thanks and lots of XXXXs and OOOOs to my husband John for his time and insightful feedback with this story—as well as his inspired preliminary cover design! I appreciate all my wonderful "peeps" in Astoria, Oregon: Meghann, Matt, Seamus, Rowan, Flora, Rosemary, Richard and Ashleigh...I'm so grateful for all the good times and adventures we've shared and for the fun to come! Big hugs for Devan Moriarty for her ideas for the book's opening. And lots of high-fives for Rowan Elfering, for the great walk around Astoria during *The Goonies'* Anniversary Celebration, and for all his suggestions and story ideas.

Many thanks as well to Lori Nelson Clonts and Lish Jamtaas for their helpful comments and input. Thank you to the E-book Formatting Fairies for designing the final book cover—amazing job, Fairies! And as always, kudos to ExperiSpence Productions for their continuing support and creative energy.

Most of all, I'm grateful to Meghan, Seamus and Rowan for inspiring this story.

Books by
Susan Colleen Browne

The Village of Ballydara Series

It Only Takes Once
A Village of Ballydara Novel, Book 1 (print and ebook)

Mother Love
A Village of Ballydara Novel, Book 2 (print and ebook)

The Hopeful Romantic
A Village of Ballydara Novel, Book 3 (ebook, soon in print)

The Secret Well
short story ebook

The Christmas Visitor
short story ebook and the sequel of *The Secret Well*

The Morgan Carey Adventure Series for Kids

Morgan Carey and The Curse of the Corpse Bride
Book 1, a lighthearted Halloween story for middle-grade readers
(print and ebook)

Morgan Carey and The Mystery of the Christmas Fairies
Book 2, a gentle fantasy novelette for middle-grade readers
(ebook, soon in print)

The Secret Astoria Scavenger Hunt
Book 3 of the Morgan Carey series, a family-friendly paranormal
chapter book for tweens (print and ebook)

Memoir

*Little Farm in the Foothills: A Boomer Couple's Search for
the Slow Life*
(print and ebook)

About the Author

Susan Colleen Browne is the creator of the Morgan Carey series for kids, as well as the Irish *Village of Ballydara* series for grownups. She's also the author of a memoir, *Little Farm in the Foothills: A Boomer Couple's Search for the Slow Life.* "Little Farm" is for dreamers of all ages, and a Washington State Library "Summer Reads" book selection. Susan is a community college creative writing instructor and lives with her husband John in the foothills of the Pacific Northwest.

When Susan isn't in the garden, she's working on her next Morgan Carey story or Village of Ballydara book!

You can contact Susan at:
www.susancolleenbrowne.com.

You'll also find recipes, book excerpts and tales from Berryridge Farm at:
www.littlefarminthefoothills.blogspot.com

Made in the USA
San Bernardino, CA
17 March 2016